D0027733

FOREVER
BIRCHWOOD

FOREVER BIRCHWOOD

Danielle Daniel

HarperCollins*Publishers*Ltd

Published by HarperCollins Publishers Ltd

First edition

HarperCollins books may be purchased for educational, business or
sales promotional use through our Special Markets Department.

HarperCollins Publishers Ltd
Bay Adelaide Centre, East Tower
22 Adelaide Street West, 41st Floor
Toronto, Ontario, Canada
M5H 4E3

www.harpercollins.ca

Library and Archives Canada Cataloguing in Publication

Title: Forever Birchwood / Danielle Daniel.
Names: Daniel, Danielle, author.
Identifiers: Canadiana (print) 20210346248 |
Canadiana (ebook) 20210346256 | ISBN 9781443463348 (softcover) |
ISBN 9781443463355 (ebook)
Classification: LCC PS8607.A55645 F67 2022 | DDC jC813/.6—dc23

Printed and bound in the United States of America
LSC/H 9 8 7 6 5 4 3 2 1

In memory of
Cindy Landry,
friends forever,
and
Sheila Barry,
for believing in me.

I carry you both in my heart.

For every child who ever swam in one of the
three hundred and thirty lakes

The City of Greater Sudbury is located within the traditional territory of the Robinson-Huron Treaty, the traditional lands of the Atikameksheng Anishnawbek and the Wahnapitae First Nations.

CHAPTER 1

ood things always happen on Saturdays. I was born
on a Saturday so I should know.

The chance of having a fun day multiplies because
some things *only* happen on this day, like Saturday morning
cartoons, meeting my friends at Birchwood and sleepovers.
But the *best* thing about Saturday is that there's still another
day before the weekend is done. So that if, for some reason,
Saturday isn't what you hope it will be, you still have Sunday
left over. A backup funday.

Saturday is also the day I spend with Grandma Houle.
Some days we play gin rummy and sip mint tea, and some
days we just weed her garden and drink large glasses of lem-
onade. Today she has an adventure planned for us that she

won't tell me much about, except that it's going to be *beyond amazing.*

From where I'm sitting on my front porch I spot her coming down the street now, zipping around the corner in her ancient grey Chevrolet. She pulls the van into our driveway and rolls down the window.

"Fancy meeting you here, Granddaughter," she calls to me. Her brown eyes are bright and her silver hair hangs in a bob, high above her shoulders.

"Funny one, Grandma," I say as I head down the walk and climb into the passenger seat. "So what is this adventure you're taking me on?"

"Somewhere I should have brought you ages ago. Buckle up, buttercup."

Just around the corner, we see Mr. Patel approaching his truck. He's dressed in his dark blue coveralls and steel-toe boots, practically our town's official uniform.

Grandma pokes her head out the window. "Happy sightseeing, Gus," she hollers as Mr. Patel hikes into his front seat. "Safe voyage down the hatch," she adds.

"Thanks, Gwen. Working a double today." He lifts his ball cap and places it back down on his head.

Grandma pats me on the knee as we pull onto the road.

"No matter how long I've lived here, I'll never understand how these miners go so long without seeing the sun. It's just not natural. Living creatures need the sun." She grips the steering wheel. "That darkness sure aged your grandpa."

"I miss him too, Grandma," I say, feeling my heart get sore. My grandpa died over a year ago and he was a miner all his life. Sometimes I wonder if Poppy would still be here if he had worked in a bank or a sporting goods store.

Grandma elbows me and gives me a glance. "Is Gus's son still in your class? Hari? He's such a kind boy."

"Yeah," I answer, though I'm glad we're almost out of the neighbourhood without seeing him. At least not right now, wearing these cut-off jean shorts and this old shirt.

We turn onto the main road where the pizza place, the tire place and the gas station are all lined up, before taking a sharp left turn that leads to the highway. As soon as we do, the mountains that surround Sudbury grow blacker before my eyes, dotted with newly planted trees and shrubs. A stranger might think things don't get enough rain or sunshine out here. But it's actually the pollution from the mines that once wiped out much of the trees and vegetation. Some areas were harder hit than others.

"There it is." Grandma nods at the Superstack. "Standing tall and always at full attention. You know, dear, I have friends who risked their lives building it, just before you were born. They were hoisted to the very top on cement buckets, of all things. Can you imagine?"

I watch the dark smoke curling up from its towering mouth into the clear blue sky. "Wow, they were so brave, Grandma," I say.

"Yes, they were."

It is the tallest smokestack in the country, maybe even in

3

the world. And Grandma is right; there have been improvements since it was built. We can swim in every lake now because there's no more acid rain falling into them. That's three hundred and thirty lakes with happy fish and clean water. That's something to be proud of.

"Wonder if I'm going to plant more trees when I'm in high school next year," I say. It's usually an entire morning or afternoon travelling on the bus, trekking with my friends, planting seedlings into the soil of the cracks in the mountain. "Way better than doing school work, that's for sure."

"Well, I hope so," Grandma replies. "There's still work to be done. You can't take from the land without giving back, and this town has a lot to make up for. Sudbury is changing for the better, but it wasn't that long ago that it was so barren it looked like the moon. Remember I told you, we even had sixteen astronauts come here to train for missions because it looked so much like a lunar landscape."

"Yup. I remember," I say.

Grandma tilts her head and gives me a wink. "Well, I'm glad we're finally doing this pilgrimage," she says. "I need to take you before I forget where the trail is."

"Yeah right. You have an excellent memory."

"Nothing lasts forever, sweet pea." She sucks in a deep breath and pushes up her sleeves. "It's still a little ways yet. Another thirty minutes if I recall."

I smile at her and lean back into my seat. "It's a nice morning for a drive."

"It sure is."

I roll my window all the way down with the wobbly silver handle, fill my lungs with pre-summer air and gaze out at the dark mountains that line both sides of our town. I spot the bushes and the trees growing within its cracks and can't help feel a happy warmth swirl in my belly. I may have been born after the regreening project started, so I don't really know exactly what the old Sudbury looked like, but I sure love the Sudbury we have today. And it's only going to get better.

Just about thirty minutes later, like Grandma said, we stop near a park with a few picnic tables. She reaches for her walking stick in the back seat while I stretch my legs and breathe in the sharp smell of the many pine trees lined up like soldiers.

"It's a good thing we left so early. It's not too hot yet. Just right for locating a very special something in the forest. That's all I'm giving away for now." She clicks her tongue.

"Grandma! You always keep me guessing! Fine." I back down, knowing she will not give in. "Lead the way, Captain." I salute her and we head off together into the brush.

We take a trail that snowmobilers use in the winter and follow the overgrown path through a maze of small poplars and white pines. The birds are singing wildly—they're probably happy it's Saturday too. After another fifteen minutes, we hold hands so I can help Grandma cross a running creek. It's a good thing she's wearing her runners instead of her usual Birkenstock sandals. As we pass another grove of pines, the trees begin to look even smaller, with thinner trunks. A line of birch trees faces us with a symmetrical row behind them. It looks like a ruler was used to separate them.

"Are these some of the newer-planted trees, Grandma? They're so different."

"Right-o. That's our regreening in plain sight. By next season, they'll be as tall as toddlers, and within no time, taller than them terrible teens." She squints and looks ahead and I can see the crinkly laugh lines around her eyes. "You know, even before the mining pollution wreaked havoc, the old-growth pines that once grew here for centuries were clear-cut and logged away. These forests have faced such destruction . . ." Her voice fades off and I notice her palm is flat against her heart. "All right, dear," she says, "let's keep going."

"But where, exactly?" I ask her. "I've never been this far into the forest before."

"Hold your wild horses," she says with a grin. "This will be worth it, I promise."

I grin back at her because her smile is always contagious, and we keep going, me trailing behind her through row after row of perfectly lined birch trees. I reach out and touch the soft white paper trunks as I pass them, their skin peeling and curling up under my fingertips.

Up ahead, Grandma stabs her stick into the ground. "Granddaughter, we have arrived!"

In front of her is what looks like another birch tree, but I'm not sure. I've never seen anything like it before. "Is it glowing?" I rub my eyes with my fists to be sure.

Grandma takes a step closer. "It does look that way, with the sun prancing on its trunk. Isn't it a beauty, Wolf? It's the loveliest shade of bronze." Grandma shields her eyes with her hand and cranes her neck back to scan the tip-top of the tree. "I can't tell you how delighted I am to set eyes on this tree after so many years."

"It's so pretty. When was the last time you saw it?"

"Well, I reckon I was around your age. Yes, I think I was your age exactly. Eleven."

I shoot her a look. "I'm twelve, Grandma. Nearly thirteen."

She chuckles. "Just making sure you're paying attention."

"Why are all the other birch trees so small and white and this one is bronze and enormous? She seems like the queen of the forest."

"She is a queen, Wolf. This tree here is a yellow birch tree. It's uncommon these days to see one, even at the edges of Sudbury's city limits. She's probably the only survivor in the area—the only one I ever found, anyways. We used to have a lot more, but the sulphur from the old smelting operations killed most of the original trees. Some forests just never grew back. The yellow birch grows very slowly—only three inches per decade—so when they regreened the area, they chose the faster-growing white birch trees instead."

"Three inches every ten years? That *is* slow."

"Precisely. And with so few around, the yellow birch became a delicacy for wildlife. The deer love to eat its seedlings and the stems are a favourite for the moose. Even beavers and porcupines like to eat its bark. I'm so glad it's still here and that the animals spared it. It's rare to see a tree like this, never mind at this grand size."

"Grandma. It's no wonder it sparkles. It's like the sole survivor of its kind." I can't help but wrap my arms around the gleaming trunk. When I do, I'm not able to reach the tips of my fingers together around the back, it's so big. The bark is soft under my cheek. It's papery thin like the white birch but with more ruffles, like the tree is wearing a special party dress. There's something comforting about being so close to it, and I breathe in a deep, earthy breath.

"I know you never met my daddy—he died long before you were ever born, even before your mother was born—but he had a real connection to trees. My daddy was able to speak tree. I wonder what this queen told him," she says, before reaching for a branch.

I look up at Grandma to be sure I heard correctly. "Speak tree, as in speak to trees?" I ask as I let go of the trunk.

"Yes. Trees spoke to him and he spoke back. My daddy believed trees felt things like we do. He said they were connected to each other and to us, and that they have stories to tell but that only some of us are lucky enough to hear them."

"But how, exactly, do they communicate?"

"He told me the trees spoke to him without using words. The words were all on the inside. Daddy told me he would put his hands on the tree and thank it for its blessings, and then he would listen carefully. If he didn't hear anything, he would ask it questions and wait for the tree to answer him. He called all the trees Tree People because our Algonquin ancestors have always believed trees possess spirits, just like us, living breathing individuals, which is why we have to treat them with kindness and love. It's a knowing that was passed down from many, many, many generations, and now I want to make sure I share it with you."

"Wow! Your dad sounds like he was a tree superhero."

Grandma rubs the trunk gently. "I guess he was. He was able to use his ability to help forests survive—like a modern-day Robin Hood for ecosystems. He knew how to tell when they were sick, so he could stop the spread of disease from one tree to the rest of its family and help them grow. He'd guide small groups into the forest and teach them how to identify trees and their leaves and indicate which ones are used in traditional medicine. That's actually why we moved from the Ottawa Valley where many of our Algonquin relatives still live. He said these northern woods called him here because they were in peril."

I'm quiet as I think about my ancestors. I love hearing Grandma talk about them. I always feel like I want to know more, because mom doesn't talk to me about this stuff, even though I ask her to. "I wish I could have known him," I say, feeling a real sadness for someone I've never met.

"Me too, sweet pea."

"But why is this the *only* yellow birch?"

Grandma stretches her neck and palms the trunk with both her hands. "I wish I could ask my daddy that question."

"What do you think he'd say?"

Grandma doesn't answer for a whole minute. I figure maybe she's trying to speak to the tree, so I just sit and wait, even though I'm not the most patient person I know. "I think he might say this tree was spared to remind us of what we lost and what we need to preserve."

I feel giant goosebumps on my skin. Truth bumps, as Grandma calls them. "Did he ever tell you what this tree said to him?"

Grandma shakes her head. "He didn't, dear. But he did tell me this: he said, *Gwenny, someday you'll come back with your own children and grandchildren, and this tree will remember you*. I actually brought your mom ages ago."

"You did?"

"Sure did. And now it's your turn." Grandma wipes her eyes before she turns around and stabs the walking stick back into the earth. "Now, why don't we have a little snack under this glorious queen, before we hit the road again? I packed some fancy peanut butter à la jelly sandwiches for us. I think she would really enjoy our company."

"That sounds perfect."

I find a shaded spot under a large branch and rest my back against its trunk. I watch a dragonfly zig and zag and zoom past me, then rise towards the tip of the splendid queen of the forest, still growing under a perfect Saturday sun.

CHAPTER 2

We head back to my house before going to Grandma's because I forgot my beading kit and I want to show Grandma the pins I've been working on. But when we turn onto my street, I spot Mom's car in the driveway.

"What is she doing home?" I say to Grandma. "Mom left way before we did this morning."

"Maybe she forgot something?"

Mom rarely forgets stuff. She's the most organized person I know.

Before we even reach the door, Mom swings it open like she's been waiting for us. She's wearing a navy and white pin-striped apron I don't remember ever seeing before.

"Betty Crocker has broken in," Grandma says, laughing at her own joke.

"Hello, Mother."

"You're really taking the open houses to a new level, wearing that." Grandma points.

Mom beams, with her hands fixed on her hips. "I'm actually home for the rest of the day!"

"You are?" I say. I don't even remember the last time we spent a Saturday together. That's when she does all her open houses to try to sell homes.

"I know. I've been working so much, I asked Lucy to fill in for me. I get to spend the rest of the day with you!"

"Well, that's super," Grandma says. "It'll be good for you two to hang out together."

"Guess so." But really, I'm not sure how I feel about this. Saturdays are for Grandma time and friend time. That's just the way it always is.

"It'll be fun." Mom pulls on my braid. "I was thinking we'd make my signature pancakes and then we could tackle a cryptic crossword puzzle, like the old days."

"It's been a long time since we did one of those," I say.

"Sounds groovy." Grandma steps into the kitchen beside me. "Though I prefer good old-fashioned jigsaw puzzles myself. Any bird puzzle will do."

"You do have quite a collection." I nod.

"C'mon, Wolf, it'll be fun. I picked up the *Northern Star* this morning." Mom lifts it up from the counter to show me. "And the pancakes won't take long to make."

"I guess," I say, hunger gnawing at my stomach, even though I had peanut butter and jelly sandwiches not long ago. Hiking must make you extra hungry.

"Well, enjoy the day, girls. I'm off to put my feet up and have some mint tea."

"Bye," I tell her, "and thanks for the ultra-fun morning." I wrap my arms around her soft body.

She bends down to touch her forehead to mine. "Fill your belly, Granddaughter. A girl's gotta eat."

"Roger that," I answer and watch her close the creaky screen door.

I saunter back to the kitchen sink and pour a glass of water.

Mom squeezes in beside me to wash her hands. "It sounds like you had a nice time."

"Uh-huh, sure did." I chug the whole glass and wipe my mouth. "We went for a long hike. We drove down the highway, all the way to the end of the city where it still looks patchy and the trees have been replanted."

"Wow, all the way out there? Well, it's no wonder she needs to lie down. She's been so tired lately," Mom says.

"I'm certain she'll be back to her regular self soon," I say. My grandma is tough and full of zest, as she calls it.

Mom starts cracking eggs and mixing the batter for the pancakes. It's pretty weird seeing her like this, even though she often made pancakes before she became a realtor. We'd even have them for supper sometimes but she would call them crepes, make them much thinner and fill them with spinach, cheese and mushrooms. Minus the mushrooms for me.

"Well, sit down already and let me whip these up."

"Okay," I say as I refill my water and move to the table.

Before I make it to my seat, the floor starts to shake under our feet. I hold on to the counter while Mom steadies the bowl full of batter. The tremor lasts about six seconds, and when it's done, we both look around quickly to make sure nothing has broken or fallen off the wall.

"Must be another mine blast," Mom says. "There sure have been a lot of them lately."

Just last week there were three in a row. And while mine blasts are a regular occurrence day or night, since we're a nickel-mining town after all, they don't usually happen this often.

Steady again, Mom turns around to the refrigerator, grabs the milk and adds it to the flour mix already in the large glass bowl. "Pass me the cinnamon, please. It's in the cupboard, next to the salt," she tells me.

I reach for it and bring it to her.

"Give it a few taps," she says. "Go ahead."

I open the small flap and tap in a few shakes of the sweet and spicy reddish-brown powder. It immediately wakes up my taste buds.

"My secret ingredient." She winks. "Now you know."

"I'm finding out lots of new things about my family this morning," I say.

Mom adds more milk to the bowl slowly, getting the batter to just the right thickness. "Oh really, like what?"

"Like that Great-Granddaddy was a tree talker."

"Oh that," she says with a slight roll of her eyes.

"Grandma says he could speak to trees and they spoke back."

Mom's jaw tightens. "Grandma says a lot of things."

"So you don't believe it?"

"I believe that she believes it."

"That's not the same thing."

She stops mixing and places her hands on either side of the bowl.

"Grandma took me out there when I was a kid, too." She wipes her hands on the front of her apron. "Sweetheart, the truth is, I don't believe in those stories, but you are free to believe in what you want."

I know she's serious because she's looking straight at me, with her head tilted forward and her eyes wide without blinking.

And even though I might regret it, I decide now is as good a time as any to ask her about something that has been bothering me.

"Why don't you think like Grandma thinks, you know, about nature and stuff?"

"I like nature," she says, like she's trying to convince me.

"I mean, well, not *just* nature. Grandma talks a lot about her culture and traditions. She wants me to learn about them, but you never talk to me about that stuff."

"It's complicated." She rubs her temple and turns around to light the stove.

"Why?"

She sighs. "It just is. Listen. Can we talk about this at another time? I really want us to have a special day together. You know, mother and daughter seizing the moment, charting our own paths!"

I cross and uncross my arms. I spy the newspaper on the counter, the flour on Mom's temple, the apron tied around her waist and the whiffs of cinnamon wafting around me.

"Fine."

Mom looks relieved. She relaxes her shoulders, and then reaches for a spatula and drops a dollop of butter into the hot pan. It spits and sizzles immediately.

"I'm sorry I've been gone so much, sweetie."

I can tell she means it. I squeeze a smile. "It's nice that you took the day off."

She kisses my cheek. "Now, let's make a giant stack."

Fifteen minutes later, Mom hands me a towering plate of pure delight. It's perfect timing. My stomach is growling like a grizzly bear.

"All we need now is the maple syrup and we are ready to feast." She opens the refrigerator door and peers in. "Oh no! I forgot the syrup. We only have the fake stuff." Mom hangs her head with disappointment and I can't help but feel a little bad.

"It'll be fine," I tell her. I get up and grab the fake syrup from the pantry, pop the top off and quickly pour it over my pancakes, and take a bite.

"They're delicious, Mom. Seriously."

She winks at me and pours some on her own pancakes. We chew in happy silence until our bellies are full.

Even without real maple syrup, this Saturday is turning out to be a really good one after all.

CHAPTER 3

Mom and I spend the rest of the day working on the cryptic crossword puzzle. We are both a little rusty but we manage to solve every clue, including the last one: "a hairstyle with a comb in it." Mom thinks of the word *honeycomb* first, which leads me to the word *beehive*, because Grandma Houle told me she used to wear her hair like that back in the old days. And with that seven-letter word, we solve the puzzle! We are pretty proud of ourselves and decide to go out for milkshakes to celebrate.

Mom also wants to stop at the video store to rent a movie for the weekend. I convince her to get *The Goonies*. I already saw it with Grandma at the drive-in when it first came out and I think Mom will like it too. Two thumbs up.

After that, we head home to look through her stash of magazines for what Mom calls "decor inspiration." She says she wants to make over my bedroom this summer, since I'm turning thirteen. I've decided I don't want a theme, though, more like an eclectic mix of colours and patterns. So we put ideas and images from the magazines inside a folder to build the mood I want. She puts everything in folders, which she neatly files inside the filing cabinet inside her tidy office. Some moms paint ceramics for fun but my mom organizes closets and drawers.

All in all, it's been a pretty great day. But there's one part of Saturday that is yet to come, and it may be my very favourite part: Birchwood with my four best friends. I knock on the bathroom door where Mom is soaking in a hot lavender bath.

"I'm meeting the girls at the cabin."

"Okay, honey. Don't be out too late," she calls. "And put some mosquito repellent on."

"I won't. And I will!" I holler over my shoulder as I race down the stairs.

I wander out under the setting sky. This is one of my favourite times of day—when people are taking their after-dinner walks with their dogs. Everything seems to be in a slower, happier motion. I take one left turn and two rights, and the smokestack pokes its head above the rooftops, carved in the sky, puffing out smoke like a long, dark veil. I think about how things have been improving around here. Still, Mom says that some people who only pass through the city think it's ugly, with so much black rock and patchy forests. I've heard this before too, from some new kids when they move here, and I've never understood it. To me, Sudbury feels like a never-ending labyrinth to explore, with lakes and mountains and rocks of all kinds! Besides, no other city was created by a billion-year-old crater slamming into the ground—only ours.

The people in our community always help each other. Like when the snowstorms roll in or somebody's dog goes missing, everyone pitches in to help. I'm also lucky to live in an area that was spared from the worst of the pollution. Around here, we have some great trees. Some giant trees, even. I breathe in the saturated greens.

Besides NASA visiting, years ago, nothing very remarkable really happens in Sudbury, unless of course you count the weekend porketta bingo. People gather at the restaurant above the curling rink, and each lucky winner goes home with a pound of meat. True story. This is why we absolutely have to create our own adventures.

I don't stop running until I reach Birchwood, my favourite place in the world. Right at the base of the mountain, among a family of five birch trees, is the most perfect cabin a group of friends could have. Last summer, after watching *The Swiss Family Robinson* during one of our sleepovers, Ann, Brandi, Penny and I became obsessed with the idea of having our very own tree house. We all worked on the design and then we scoured our homes for building materials. And, well, maybe it's not a tree house, but it's the next best thing. The walls are mostly made out of plywood and boards, and we added a roof built from metal scraps from Brandi's dad, which covers us from the rain. We even managed to find a carpet that Ann's mom was going to donate. It's green, looks like fake grass, and it covers the dirt floor, which makes it cleaner and cozier inside.

Birchwood is the best hangout for so many reasons. The most magical things have happened here. It's where we pour our hearts out and spend time together or alone, reading, dreaming and getting away from everything. It's where we go when things go wrong too, like after Penny's brother died or when I feel sad about Poppy, or when our parents argue about stuff, and when Mom and Grandma argue too. It's where we promised each other to be best friends forever, no matter what. Hand to heart.

After we built it, we made a pact: me and Ann, Brandi and Penny meet at Birchwood every Saturday, rain or shine. At least until the arctic winter arrives and the snow is too deep to walk through. When even snowshoes can't get us there in the middle of winter, we move our meetings indoors, to Brandi's basement. We have her place to ourselves because her mom works nights at the hospital and her dad plays poker with the guys down at the Legion after his shift.

The other fun thing we started at Birchwood was to make new pins lined with tiny glass beads to attach to our shoelaces—proof of our gatherings. I like it because it's a way to express the passage of time, but with a twist and with more meaning because we choose colours that echo the season or the things we do together. I can fit about twelve pins per shoe. Once we fill the laces, we line the pins along the bottom edge of our pencil cases. Ann says it's a way to mark a milestone, like the boys do when they get their stupid badges in the boy scouts. They always flaunt their latest patch like it's a superhero crest or something. Well, except for Hari. Hari doesn't really brag like the other boys.

I stop for a second before scooting into our cabin. I notice tracks on the ground, probably caused by a four-wheeler. I look on and see many of them crisscrossing over each other, looping towards the mountain. They weren't here last week. I hope we won't have to deal with these motorized machines during the summer. We love the fact that we have this whole place to ourselves. I turn my attention to the family of five birch trees, which feel more special now, after my morning hike with Grandma. I move forward towards the biggest tree. "Hello there," I say out loud, awkwardly. Then I close my eyes and tell it my name, but only with my thoughts.

Hi, I'm Wolf Lagacé. My grandma Houle gave me the nickname Wolf after my dad named me Wilhelmina, after his favourite grandmother. Everyone just calls me Wolf, and I prefer that anyway. I've never told you this, but I'm really happy you're here, with the other trees. Thanks for growing so tall and strong, so we can have this cabin.

Then I wait. I try not to move. I listen so hard for it to say something back that I nearly forget to breathe. And then suddenly, the loudest mosquito zings in my ear and breaks my concentration. I open my eyes and shrug. "Next time," I tell the tree and rub its trunk before stepping inside the cabin.

The first thing I do is flip on the battery lantern hanging on a small hook. It fills the space with a soft, warm light. It's not very big in here, but we have an old telephone table Grandma Houle donated that we use as a desk. It has an attached seat and a drawer to store papers and pens. We like to fill it with candy, though it never stays there for long. Most importantly, we have a reading area with a beanbag chair and a bunch of cushions, along with a large stack of Archie comics that belonged to Penny's brother, some of Ann's books on the ancient Aztecs, my beloved Judy Blume books and Brandi's Baby-Sitters Club collection. She's read them all twice.

I lie down against a cushion and look through the skylight above me, grateful for the little window Brandi's dad inserted to see the night sky. The North Star is already shining bright, even though the sky is still blue. It really is a pretty picture.

I hear twigs snap under wheels and I know Ann is here. She's always the next one to arrive after me. Then Brandi and Penny usually come together, since they live two houses from each other.

I slide the wooden panel open and stick my head out the door. "Hi!"

"Big surprise! You're here first." Ann flicks down her kickstand.

"Always," I say and scooch to the back.

She flips her long, red braids behind her back. "So, what's new?"

"A lot, actually. I had an interesting morning with my grandma. We went exploring to the outer edges of town, and let's just say I found out that I am the great-granddaughter of a tree talker."

"Tree talker? Seriously? Tell me everything." Ann quickly clambers in and ducks her head but manages to knock over the stack of comic books anyway. Ann is always bumping into things.

"Grandma Houle stuff," I tell her. "I have to say, she keeps my life interesting."

"Who needs TV when you have a Grandma Houle?"

"Exactly. Not that you ever needed a TV."

Ann wipes her glasses with the bottom of her shirt and peers through them to make sure they are spotless. She combs through her bangs with her fingers. "Nope, and my new set of Encyclopedia Britannicas with gold-sided pages are keeping me busy enough. A to E so far. I'm hoping to get F to L by the end of the summer."

"You're such a nerd," I say with a big smile.

When she smiles back, it seems to stretch to her earlobes. "You can count on it."

Ann is the nicest know-it-all I know and she's told me stuff she's never told anyone else, like how she hates having red hair because everyone calls her Anne of Green Gables. But I've known Ann since our moms put us in the same tap-dance class when we were five. My Ann (without the *e*) reminds me of an owl (sure and steady) and the other Anne, from Green Gables, reminds me of a flamingo (animated and theatrical). Two entirely different birds.

I hear the ticking of a bike slowing down and poke my head out the door.

"We're here!" Penny hollers at me while Brandi jumps off the back of her bike and does a cartwheel.

"Sorry we're late," Brandi says when she's right-side up again.

Ann shouts behind me: "Hurry up and get in here before the bugs do!"

Penny lets her bike fall against a tree and rushes the door. Once inside, Ann ends up sitting at the telephone desk and I take the cushions with Penny, while Brandi plops herself into the beanbag chair.

"Just another 'Sudbury Saturday Night,'" Brandi giggles. She leans back and stretches out her legs. "Is this place getting smaller?"

Almost on cue, the garland of yellow and purple pompoms we made falls from the ceiling and lands across our laps.

We all start laughing.

"Now *that* was a coincidence." Ann points. "We're just getting bigger, you brainiac."

"Okay," I lean in. "Now that we're all here, let's recite our pledge." Last year we made a promise to take this seriously and treat this like a real club with a code of honour.

"Of course," Brandi says. "We have protocol. Standards, people."

Ann slides the door open. "Okay, let's take it outside then, under the open sky."

Now, standing in a small circle, we start:

> *One, two, three, four,*
> *Together today and forevermore.*
> *Friendship first, always true,*
> *Northern Star lead us through.*

"Wolf, I seriously love this pledge," Penny says with a pale light across her cheeks.

I smile an extra-long smile.

CHAPTER 4

S o, what's the plan tonight? Anyone manage to snag that tea-leaf reading book from the library yet? I can't believe how popular it is."

Penny's blue eyes look green in this light. She's always reminded me of a Cabbage Patch Kid with those big eyes, round cheeks and frilly clothes. I was obsessed with those dolls when they first came out. Mom stood in line for hours before the store even opened so I could get one for Christmas one year. We were all obsessed with our dolls back then. We used to bring them everywhere we went. Now, I can't remember the last time we talked about dolls, never mind brought them along.

"Nope. Still not available," Brandi says. "Last I checked, anyway."

I square my shoulders. "I thought we'd take a hike up the mountain, to see where those tracks might lead, the ones crossing from the bottom of the hill."

"Good idea," Ann says. "I noticed them on the way up. They look like tractor tracks, but why would there be construction way out here?"

"It seems super strange," Penny agrees.

"Maybe it's alien undercover stuff." Brandi grabs the flashlight she brought and makes a scary face.

"It would make for a memorable night," I say.

Ann and Brandi giggle, though Penny is already chewing her pink nails. I remember when we used to all hate pink.

"So, should we just get going then?" Ann sprays mosquito repellent on her neck and ankles.

Brandi floods the path with the warm glow of the flashlight. "I'm kind of hoping we see Bigfoot or something."

"Let's not start again," I warn her. "Last week you were hoping for UFOs. You really need to stop watching late-night TV."

"It's my sister. She's been filling my head with this bizarro stuff." Brandi's sister is in college, in the local dental hygienist program. Brandi says she only watches scary movies or anything that's on *Dateline* or *W5*, and she controls the TV.

Penny makes her way in between Brandi and me. "My brother used to believe in all that. But it's always kind of freaked me out."

Brandi and I share a glance, and I slow my pace so Penny can walk between us. Penny's gotten even more sensitive and fearful of things since her brother died. He was killed by a drunk driver last year coming back from a Sudbury Wolves hockey game. The whole town had just celebrated a huge win, scoring at the buzzer to beat the Soo Greyhounds. And then, the next day, as the town was just barely waking up, news of Scott's death spread like wildfire. It was the saddest day. Everybody says he was way too young. Penny's dad is the only one in our group who doesn't work in the mines, which you would think would keep their family safe. He's an accountant and works all day in a clean office, which is almost the opposite of a miner. Brandi and Ann's dads are both miners. I guess my dad doesn't work in the mines either, not anymore. Not that I ever knew him. He moved away when I was just a baby, and I guess I just got used to him not being here. Poppy was more like my dad, which is why it hurt so much when he passed away.

"Well," Ann says, "I hate to burst your paranormal bubble, but we've spent enough time in the woods, and I think one of us would have seen an eight-foot hairy beast by now if Bigfoot did exist. Not to mention that there is no current scientific evidence that supports humanoid creatures living in forests. New discoveries are extremely rare because most findings cannot be supported with any quantitative data."

Brandi shakes her head and laughs. "You always keep it real."

We continue moving upward past a row of trees glowing under the early moonbeams. I love that summer is almost here, even though I always forget how many bugs it brings with it. They're already chomping at my elbows and ankles.

"Ann! Please tell me you brought that bug repellent?"

"Sorry, I left it at the cabin."

"Great." I slap at my skin and pick up the pace.

It's still warm out, even with the sun now behind the mountain. The days are getting longer and summer holidays are starting soon. Very soon—only two more weeks of school to go. I've been going to Rockwood my whole life, junior and senior.

We keep trekking up the gravel path and get to the part of the clearing where the trees are more spread out and the tracks more visible. They look like four-wheeler tracks to me, but maybe Ann is right, maybe they are more like tractor tracks. They're deep, so whatever the machine is, it's heavy.

"What are we looking for, exactly?" Brandi's twirling a curl around her finger. I can tell she's ready to move on to the next thing. Brandi gets her curls from her dad. He's from Barbados and immigrated here to work in the mines. We became immediate friends when she arrived in grade five because we both collected rocks and gemstones. But these days, she's ditched the stones and prefers to obsess about Denis Gervais.

"Well, anyone else want to head back to the cabin? I need to get your opinion on something." She spins to face us.

"Or someone," Penny says, in a teasing way.

"Denis Gervais will have to wait," Ann answers, visibly annoyed. "We need to find out why these tracks are here."

"Yeah. What she said." I nod to Ann. "There's so many of them. I want to know what's going on here." We continue to follow the marks up the mountainside, towards the lookout where you can see Ramsey Lake, our city's ninth-largest body of water. Our biggest lake, Lake Wanapitei, is actually in the *Guinness Book of World Records* for being the world's largest lake located totally within a single city. Another feather in our cap, Grandma would say. She told me that Ramsey Lake was originally called Bitimagamasing, which means water that lies on the other side of the hill. Her Ojibway friends told her that. The lake's name was eventually changed by the settlers, like most of the other names of nearby towns and lakes. Grandma says the settlers removed them all, one by one, until no trace of the Ojibway language was seen or heard, like it never existed. She also says that one day, and one day soon, these names should all be changed back because it's the right thing to do; that just because you change a name to something, it doesn't make it yours.

As we turn around the next bend of trees, I see something catch the light across the valley. Something that looks like it's floating. Something unnaturally bright, like neon orange.

"What is that?" I say.

Penny pulls up to a stop behind me. "What? What is it?" she asks, a little nervously.

We gradually reach the top of the ridge and I see them clearly now. Orange plastic bands, flapping in the wind. "Do you see them, tied around the pines?" I point into the distance.

"Yeah, I totally do," Brandi says, "but why?"

"I've never seen those here before," Ann says.

"Me neither." A knot tightens in my stomach. "Let's get a closer look." I pick up the pace, and then we're right in front of the banded pine trees and I'm very confused.

Brandi reaches out and pokes at one of the bands. "Why are so many trees wrapped like this?"

"Maybe they're sick?" Penny asks.

"They don't look sick," I say. "They're big and healthy." And they really are. These pines are taller than a house and nearly touching the sky.

"Whoa, you guys, look! These ones over here have Xs spray-painted on them," Brandi cries from where she's moved around the path.

I feel like I'm seasick but on land. This is not good news.

Brandi stands on her tippytoes. "This doesn't look good and I'm not talking aliens here."

"Nope. It's not aliens." I finally say the words out loud. "They're clear-cutting this land," I tell them.

"You mean, chopping the trees down to build new construction?" Brandi frowns.

Ann sighs. "Yes, exactly. I wasn't sure at first, but this is what I was afraid of. It's happened before."

I feel a sharp stone in my throat. I turn and face Brandi. "They'll need to build a road to get access." My breath is shallow, but I continue. "And Birchwood is at the base of the mountain. It will be in their way."

"No! They can't do that!" Penny cries.

"But why would anyone bother building up here?" Brandi gestures around us. "It's like no man's land."

"For the views," Ann says. "You can see the whole town from up here."

We stare down into the basin, where street lights blink and red tail lights flash below. Beyond the lights, the lake gleams and glistens, stretching from one end of the city to the other. And above it, the stars twinkle and the moon hangs perfectly in the setting sky, illuminating the lake like it's a painting, like everything you need is right here. My stomach wobbles again. The thought of losing all these trees makes my insides shake like a chain of mine blasts.

"This just . . . we can't let them do this." Ann looks angry. Before I can stop her, she marches to the closest spruce, reaches up and rips off its orange band. But then she just stands there with it gripped in her hand. I wonder if she's surprised at what she just did.

I'm mad too. But I feel frozen. I just don't understand why anyone would think it was a good idea to cut down any of Sudbury's trees. It's taken so long to get new ones to grow and try to make the city green again. "Why plant trees on the mountain just to cut others down? It doesn't make sense."

"That's for sure." Brandi throws a rock down the mountain. I count eight seconds before we hear it land in the bushes below.

"So many things don't make sense," Ann says.

I glance up at the starry sky and all I can think about now is the majestic queen birch I saw with Grandma Houle. How my great-granddaddy made sure to protect it, so I could see it someday. Then, I think of the family of five birch trees that encircles our cabin, our most treasured place. We could lose them. I stare at the beautiful trees that surround us—the Tree People.

"We have to do something," I say quietly.

Ann looks at me. "You're right," she says. She turns to face all of us. "This is environmental destruction. Do you know how many ecosystems are on this mountain alone?"

"Birchwood is my favourite place ever," Penny says. "We need to save it. I can't lose anything else."

Brandi reaches over and puts an arm around her. "It's our super-special spot. And, besides, where else would we hang out?"

"And explore," I say.

"Stargaze," Ann says.

"Share our secrets," Penny says.

"Yup. Pretty much do everything," Brandi says.

"We need to do whatever it takes to save it. We have to." Suddenly I need to get away from the orange Xs. It feels like they're screaming at me from the trees.

We hurry along and make our descent. The mosquitoes are getting vicious and stinging me behind the ears.

When we reach the bottom, Penny stops in place, with her eyes wide open like two full moons. "So, what are we going to do?"

"Let's each come up with some ideas and meet here tomorrow so we can make a plan," I say, because my brain can't process anything else right now.

"Okay. Works for me. You want a seater home?" Ann swats at the swarming bugs.

"Definitely." I need to escape this biting frenzy. I climb onto Ann's bike and fold my arms around her waist. Brandi gets behind Penny on her Supercycle and none of us say a word as we ride down and away from the mountainside. I feel the warm breeze against my cheeks and count every single tree we pass, as I try to keep my feet from hitting the ground while Ann steers us over the bumps.

CHAPTER 5

I wake to the hum from the weekend lawn mowers buzzing in my ears. The scent of freshly cut grass floats through my open window and Mr. Vaillancourt's fancy sprinklers ra-ta-tat, six doors down. The bright morning sun pokes through my curtains as last night comes spiralling back to me. I roll over and press my forehead against the wall's cool surface. I wish we could have seen Bigfoot or even a UFO. Anything else but those blazing oranges Xs. I can hear Mom in the kitchen downstairs. I'm surprised she's home again this morning, after missing yesterday's open house. Maybe she's just baking a batch of chocolate chip cookies for today's viewings, so the new houses smell like real homes. Grandma says burning sage would work better than cookies, but Mom's never been convinced. Just thinking about cookies makes my stomach grumble, so I force myself out of bed and make my way down the stairs, slowly, like a snail.

"There you are!" Mom says. She's fully dressed in a white blouse and grey slacks. "Aren't you a sleepyhead this morning?"

"Morning." I yawn. "Shouldn't you be at work by now?"

"I decided to go wild and take the entire weekend off." Her eyes twinkle like two bright stars.

"You're a real party animal, Mom," I joke as I reach for the cereal box. "Seriously, though, what's going on? You never take a whole weekend off."

"Well, if you must know, things have been going really well at work. I actually have a big new project lined up and I think this summer is going to be a great one for us."

I stare at her. I think about the trees that are marked for destruction, most likely soon to be replaced by new homes, and my words dislodge and tumble out like my cereal into the bowl, loose and wobbly. I feel like it's her fault. Ever since my mom became a real estate agent, it seems like she's forgotten what has to happen for those new homes to be built.

"Why can't you sell houses that already exist? Old ones."

"Not this again." She rolls her eyes like I knew she would.

But I'm not ready to let this go. "Remember Westmount Park? It had the best bike routes and now it's totally gone. And half the class had to change schools thanks to the new zoning. Every time a new subdivision is built, something changes."

"The town is growing and we need to build new homes to support it. All of us need to sacrifice, even you," she says and then looks down into her coffee, both hands clasped around the yellow mug.

"Grandma says stories live in old things. Why would someone want a house with no soul anyways? No stories?"

Mom sighs as she stands up to refill her cup. "You and Grandma both know that new things eventually become old things."

"Whatever. I'll never build a new house, not when it means taking away animal homes. Not when older ones can be fixed."

"You're too young to understand."

"I am not! I do understand."

"This is my job."

"Sure, your job is to help think up catchy names for new neighbourhoods, like Safe Haven Gardens, Blue Jay Trails or Cardinal Way. But the thing is, you really don't seem to care about birds or gardens."

"Sweetheart, you need to see the whole picture," she says, now loading glasses into the dishwasher. "We're providing jobs, growing our population. It's good for the city."

"There has to be another way." I grab the milk and splash it in my bowl, wishing for once she would see it my way.

"This is how I pay the bills." She snaps the dishwasher closed and cranks it on. "I'm a single parent and I need to support this family." She crosses her arms in a giant X.

It's always just been me and my mom, and I know it *is* all on her to pay the bills, but my heart still floods with frustration, even so.

She pulls on the cuffs of her sleeves. "Well, on another note, I think you should get your hair cut today. Don't you think it's way overdue?" She tilts her head to the side and stuffs her hands in her pockets.

I can't find any more suitable words so I just stare at her hair, which sits in a perfectly coiffed tight bun. Her pressed pants, the crease like a line in the sand.

"Fine," is all I can muster.

Maybe I should come back with a bun in my own hair and see if she'll nitpick that too. I leave my soggy cereal on the counter. I rush to my room, flop myself on the bed and squeeze my eyes shut, blocking out the light while my stomach grumbles with total starvation. I roll over on my mattress and press my forehead against the cool wall once again.

The thing is, I like being alone on weekends. I prefer it. Well, most of the time. Grandma Houle is just a few roads over on Hawthorne. I used to have to go there all of the time, especially before I took my babysitting course last summer. But now, Mom lets me stay home alone.

I hope she goes back to work. At least that will feel normal.

❧

The phone rings four times before I realize my mom isn't going to pick it up. I race downstairs to the kitchen to grab it on the wall. I wish she would just let me have a telephone in my room.

"Hello?" I say, slightly out of breath.

"Wolf, it's Ann. I barely slept last night, thinking about Birchwood."

"I know."

"Listen. I've done some research on those orange flags and I think we were right. They're going to remove every tree that has one."

"How do you know?"

"I called my uncle Bill, who works construction, and he flat-out told me."

"You're sure?"

"Positive. He knows everything about zoning and construction."

"This is terrible news." I lean against the wall and twirl the curly black cord, getting my finger stuck in the coils. "Honestly, I really don't know what to do about this yet, but I've been informed by the matriarch that I need a haircut, so do you want to come with me and we can brainstorm a little before we meet up with the others?"

"Sure! I just have to swing by the library first to drop off some books."

I run a quick calculation in my head. I'll have to shower, get dressed and eat something . . . "Okay, I'll meet you there in an hour and then we can head to the mall."

"Perfect. I'll see you there," Ann says.

As I hang up the phone, I spot Mom's note on the counter.

*Gone grocery shopping. Be back soon. Don't forget to
get your hair trimmed.*

Love, Mom

I scoot upstairs to shower. When I catch my reflection in
the mirror, I realize my mom is right. My hair is extra big these
days and I don't think it's ever been this long. It reaches the
middle of my back now and this almost-summer weather is
making it feel super heavy. It smells funky too, like pine cones
and sulphur and leaves.

After a hot shower, I brush my hair into a large braid and eat
a gigantic bowl of Cap'n Crunch. Then I hightail it to meet Ann.

As I approach the library, I see Ann locking up her bike
near the cedar hedge. She grabs her books from her basket and
meets me at the front doors.

"So, what have you been reading these days?" I look under
her elbows and spy the titles: *Solar Eclipses and Other Phenom-
ena* and *The Secret Mummies in Ancient Egypt.* "Interesting reading material."

"Thanks," she says, like it's the most normal thing in the
world to be reading about that stuff in her free time.

"But, seriously though, do you ever read fiction?"

"Nope," she answers, unapologetically. "I leave the make-
believe books for you."

We walk through the set of double front doors and zip
straight to the front desk to drop off Ann's books. I notice right
away that Ms. Barry is there. Sitting tall with perfect posture,

her hair slicked back in a small French twist. Her shoulders are puffed up with massive shoulder pads and she's stamping a large stack of new books with military precision.

"The battleaxe is here," I whisper behind my hand.

"She's never not here," Ann whispers back. "She must live in a secret room behind the walls or something."

"I can totally picture that." I try not to giggle.

"You just made it, Ms. McFadden," Ms. Barry says, without slowing down her perfect stamping rhythm.

Thwack.

Thwack.

"They're not late," Ann says.

"Just about," Ms. Barry quips. "You don't want to be on the tardy list. That could lead to other unbecoming behaviour, like your dog eating your homework." She smiles her librarian smile.

Thwack.

"I've seen that slippery slope in action."

Thwack.

Thwack.

Thwack.

"On time is on time," I say, wanting to support Ann.

"Ms. Lagacé." Her head swings towards me. "When was the last time you borrowed a book from the library?" She leans forward, holding her rubber stamp mid-air.

I flash her a long, sheepish grin and take a small step back. "Have a nice summer, Ms. Barry."

"Freeze!" she says, deep, from her throat. She's holding up her large hand, the one not holding the stamp.

We don't move. Or breathe. I stop mid-step.

"Please back up," she says.

We creep backwards, very slowly, without even turning our heads.

"Ann," she says, "I have set aside these books for you, about the Mayans. They're new and I know you'll enjoy them."

"Oh, that's nice of you, thank—"

"Wolf—"

"Yes." I try to stop my eyes from bugging out.

"Judy Blume's latest. Sign it and go."

"Oh! I was hoping to read that. How did you—"

"I just know," she says, eyeballing us.

"Thank you," I squeak out, wishing I didn't like books with characters who feel so true because I'm totally giving in and scribbling my name on the card.

Ms. Barry stamps both cards and we blast out of there.

"Ugh! Why does that lady freak me out so much?" I say, once we're through the glass doors. "Even when she's kind of nice."

"She does it on purpose," Ann says. "I think she likes to be the boss of everyone. Like she knows everything about everything."

"It's so annoying."

"Seriously."

"Wait a minute, that sort of sounds like someone I know," I say, nudging her as we dump our books in her bike basket.

"Funny one," Ann says, nudging me back before I get on her bike.

We take off together through the trail lined with black-eyed Susans, which leads to the mall. It's a shortcut that shaves off about ten minutes that we're pretty sure no one else knows about. Our foursome has a monopoly on all the hidden paths in this town. We start to slow the pace as the sun beats down on us.

"So," I say over her shoulder, "I was thinking about Birchwood. Maybe we should remove those orange bands from the trees. You know, the ones you already started ripping down." I can't help but smirk remembering Ann being so bold.

"Yeah, I kind of can't believe I did that."

"Seriously though, maybe if we remove them all, they won't know which trees to cut down."

"That's a good start. Then we need to find out exactly who is doing this. It'll be easier to create a plan once we know who we're dealing with," Ann says.

"Exactly."

CHAPTER 6

My hands feel sweaty as we step inside Chez Mimi. And as I look around the bright, mirrored hair salon, with the dazzling lights shining down on me, I have this deep, inner sense that I need to do something different. Since I'm turning thirteen real soon, this feels like the *perfect* time to be bold and get the haircut I've always wanted. Even though I have a non-stop feeling mom won't like it.

Hair has always been a big deal in my family. Grandma says braids connect us to our ancestors and to our own spirit. She used to have very long hair, but a year after Poppy died, she chopped it off. She said it was a way to ensure Poppy's spirit travelled safely home and that she was ready to let go of all the heaviness in her heart, after so many months of sorrow.

Grandma said it was a special way to honour him, and the cycle of life.

I've always worn my hair in braids. In grade four, Gregory K. started calling me Pocahontas, which really bugged me but I never gave in. I kept wearing my hair in braids all through grades four *and* five. Ann said he was beyond ignorant. I only started wearing banana clips in grade six because it was faster to put my hair up for gym class. I still wear braids a lot.

Grandma says that cutting your hair is a sacred event—that it shouldn't be taken lightly and that your reasons should always be important. Something very strong inside my heart is telling me to do this today. Like change *must* happen. Like I want my insides and outsides to match and somehow this haircut is part of that.

I wait my turn and eventually climb into the black vinyl chair, and a hairdresser wearing a name tag that reads *Carla*, with streaks of purple in her spikey hair, bounces my way. The radio is playing that new song I love, "I Think We're Alone Now" by Tiffany something, and she's dance-walking to it.

When Carla asks me what I want to do, I exhale and scrounge up my bravery. "Cut it off," I hear myself say with a slight quiver in my voice. The blue satin cape now cinched around my neck.

Ann looks up from her book, stunned, while Carla puts down a pair of sharp scissors.

"Listen, sugar, as much as I'd like to do something different for a change, I'm not sure I'm comfortable chopping off your extremely long hair without a parent present."

"You can't undo this," Ann says, standing behind me all of a sudden. "Seriously," she whispers at me.

"I know"—I feel some uneasiness swell again—"but I need to. I *should* be the boss of my own hair, and besides, I don't want to fuss with it anymore." This is something I can control, and that part feels important to me right now.

Carla snaps her gum, still hesitating.

"It's my hair and my decision, and I want it off," I proclaim, smoothing out my cape. "Please."

"Look, why don't I give you a shoulder-length cut, and then if you want to go shorter, come back next week and I'll take some more off, no charge."

"Nope. I'm ready now." My feet are steady against the metal footrest attached to the chair. I went into this shaky at first, but now I'm one hundred percent positive about my decision.

"I see I have a determined chica in my chair today. You're on!" She gives me a thumbs-up.

Ann hides her face in her hands and doesn't look up until my long braid has been snipped off. I pick it up and can't help but feel pure exhilaration. Carla keeps cutting my hair until I am left with the shortest haircut I've ever had since I was probably two years old—a pixie cut.

Carla snaps her gum again and twirls me around in the

chair to face her. "I hope you don't regret it, 'cause you look totally ace!"

I jump up to my feet and tilt my face towards the mirror. I look older. Stronger. "I love it." I spin around and face Ann. "What do you think?"

"It totally suits you! You kinda look like a famous actress. I really love it."

"I do too!" I say, feeling like a new and improved me.

"You look cool, kid," Carla says, before I stride to the cashier to pay.

"Thanks," I answer, my heart overflowing with pride.

"Is your mom going to freak when she sees you?" Ann says. "I mean, I like it, but it's a drastic change, you know?"

"Well, she did want me to cut it," I say hesitating. "I'll just explain to her how I *needed* to do this."

I run my hand against the back of my neck, feeling it bare and exposed, light and free. Somehow, I seem even taller with this short hair.

"I need to get home, Wolf, but good luck. I hope she likes it as much as me," Ann says as she swings her long ponytail over her shoulder and hops on her bike.

"Me too," I say, but I think I know exactly what Mom will think about this pixie cut. I swallow a growing lump in my throat.

"Oh! Here's your book." Ann hands it to me and takes off.

The clouds are crowding in the sky while I pinch the book in my hands, thinking this just might be an actual real-life Judy Blume moment.

Car in driveway. Check.

I see my reflection in the small window of the door and regret my decision for a microsecond. It is a ginormous change. I can't believe I actually did it. But it felt right. It felt necessary and it's *my* hair. I push my shoulders back. Swing open the door.

"I'm home! Mom? Where are you?" I lay the braid on the kitchen counter, but I keep the book in my hands.

"In the basement. Laundry room!"

"Coming down!"

My heart is pounding inside my throat and my palms feel extra clammy. And then there's Mom, loading the drum with her back to me.

"I'm right behind you."

"Sorry, I forgot to put this in the wash and—oh no! Your hair? What did you do?" She drops the blouse onto the floor. Pastes both hands against her mouth.

"Don't you love it?" I spin around, all ten fingers dancing at the nape of my neck.

She steps back. "Oh, Wolf," she says, her eyes filling with tears.

"Mom—" I falter.

"I was expecting a trim, a couple of inches at the most," she says.

I thought she'd be upset but I didn't think she'd cry. "It's just hair! It's not permanent!"

"I'm . . . surprised," she says. "This is such a radical change. Why didn't you tell me you wanted to go so short? Your hair was so beautiful, Wolf. So long. It will take years to grow it back out."

"Well"—my voice starts to shake—"when I was sitting there in the chair, I just had this really deep feeling inside that I *needed* to do this, for me. You've always encouraged me to do what feels right and this felt right, Mom." My words hang above us in the air, along with the clothes dangling on the basement clothesline, her fancy blouses scattered across, kept in place by wooden pins.

"Okay. Of course. It suits you," she finally says, biting down on her bottom lip. "I mean, if anyone can carry this look, it's you." She nods her head, then reaches for my short hair.

A feeling of pride swells up in my chest and my shoulders finally relax. I didn't realize they were so high and tense, like nearly touching my ears. I pivot to run up to my bedroom, then Mom trumpets behind me: "Get ready, we're going to Grandma's for dinner. She's expecting us."

I sprint up the stairs, bounding two steps at a time.

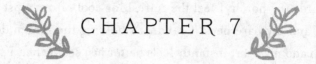

CHAPTER 7

We haven't said a word to each other the whole way to Grandma Houle's. Even though she's not mad about my haircut, there's something different between us. Of course the radio is still broken so we're riding in uncomfortable silence. Saturday's tasty pancakes and successful crossword session feel like another era. I'm holding the store-bought lemon meringue pie in my lap while Mom steers us down the road in our beige K-car with a beige interior. The rain is falling hard and fast against the windshield, and with every tree I see along the way, my mind keeps rushing back to the orange flags and what they might mean for Birchwood. When Mom stops the car, I rip off my seatbelt and push open the rusty door.

"Be careful not to slip in the driveway. I can take the pie in," she says.

"I can do it." I push the car door shut with my hip and hurry towards the porch. I feel the refreshing cool rain against my face and my bare neck. Grandma's holding the screen door open and my heart instantly feels better just seeing her. I step inside and hand her the pie.

"Wow, who's the babe?" She winks at me.

"Grandma!" I feel my face flush.

Mom races behind me for shelter and then unzips her high-heeled boots. The kind that reach your knees.

Grandma nods. "We've got a model in our midst."

"Mother, really?"

"Can't an old lady tell her granddaughter she's beautiful?"

I kick off my shoes and let the smallest smile slip from my lips.

"What precipitated this grand transformation? Is it a political statement? Some kind of standoff I should know about? You're not fasting to protest animal cruelty, are you? Fill me in, Granddaughter."

"Nothing like that. I just *really* needed a change, like my long hair no longer felt like me anymore."

"I see. Well, dear, it's important to honour those feelings. Change is good. It's necessary. Absolutely. Positively. No change, no growth."

I flash a whole smile, teeth and all.

"You have always been your own person and that is the best way to be. Not to mention, with Solstice and the new moon approaching, as well as your impending thirteenth birthday, this is an ideal time for such a profound change."

I prance around the kitchen on the balls of my feet.

"Right, Cathy?" Grandma hands mom an iced tea.

I watch Mom searching for something in the fridge; she's shuffling things around, shoving the Tupperware from side to side. She then opens a couple of drawers and doors. "Where's your cutting board? Why don't you keep it in on the counter like everyone else?"

"It's where it always is, tucked here right beside the micro-wave. You'd know that if you came around more than once in a blue moon."

Mom spots the cutting board and places it on the counter, and we all fall into line.

"Granddaughter, can you grab the cucumbers from the crisper and the green onions too?"

I do as I'm instructed, and pretty soon we're all working in silence next to each other. All I hear is the clock ticking on the wall. I peel the cucumber, Mom chops it in thin circles and Grandma makes a design on the dinner plate with the green onions placed like sunrays and then she adds the slices of tomato to fill the centre.

"What should we call this one?" she asks me.

"What about Van Gogh's Garden Patch or Emily Carr's Veg-etable Virtuoso," I say, grateful for Mr. Gooding's grade seven art class.

"I like the way you think," Grandma says. "Let's go with Emily Carr! We could use her moxie in this room." She glances at Mom. "That woman wasn't afraid of anything or anyone, painting and writing in the woods by herself all those years. Some people would call her a misfit, but I see her as a pioneer for women and conservationism."

Mom continues to set the table, mostly ignoring her.

"She was a writer as well. You should read her autobiography someday, Wolf."

"I'll add it to my list."

We take our seats at the table. Grandma offers us each a cloth napkin and we lay them across our laps like we're in a restaurant. "Did you girls hear about that new UFO sighting down by Copper Cliff mines?" she asks.

"Oh, come on, you know that stuff's not real," Mom says.

"I know, I know, we've got a skeptic in our midst, don't we?" Grandma winks at me. "Well, I think anything's possible, in fact I hope it's real. The more the merrier, I say. This world is full of things we don't understand, Cathy, and thank goodness. It keeps things exciting."

We smile at each other and Mom keeps her head down and chews with great concentration. Sometimes I think Grandma and me are the exact same, minus the years between us. I like to think that anything is possible too. Not that I want to see any small green men in my town, but an open mind is way more fun than not believing in things you can't understand.

The rest of dinner is mostly talking: Grandma about her garden and the infestation of earwigs (so gross), Mom

dodging questions about work (because of Birchwood, I wonder?) and stories about how Auntie Beth is trying to live off
the grid in North Bay (she's vegetarian) and how Uncle Kevin
is working sixty hours a week at the *Toronto Star* (Grandma
calls him a city slicker). This kind of talk is not that stimu-
lating to me, and my mind starts drifting again to the painted
orange Xs. I've got to figure out how the girls and I are going to
get more information about Birchwood's possible demolition.
My heart hurts just thinking about it, but it turns out I wasn't
the only one who couldn't be at the cabin tonight. Brandi and
Ann had family dinners too, and Penny is too afraid to go by
herself.

Once dinner's over, Grandma hands us large slices of
lemon meringue pie on her olive green plates, and after she
sits down, I can tell she wants to say something and that she's
trying to find the right words, because she's acting really quiet
and uncomfortable, which is totally rare for her. Mom is busy-
ing herself by pouring more iced tea.

Finally, Grandma puts her fork down and comes out with
it. "Girls, it's Poppy's birthday next Sunday, and I was wondering if you'd come fishing with me in his honour?" She
pauses. "You know, by the creek, the one he used to walk to
every day after work. It would be a great way to keep his memory alive."

My mom wipes her mouth. "I probably have to work. Especially since I just took the whole weekend off." She wipes her
mouth with her napkin again.

"It would mean a lot to me. We can pack a picnic lunch and it would be a nice afternoon together."

I hold my breath while Mom pushes the lemon custard on her plate. She takes a large sip from her glass, swallows with great effort and says, "All right, I'll find a way to be there."

"Super!" Grandma snaps her hands together.

We finish our pie and don't stay much longer after dinner.

Mom says I need to get to bed because I have school in the morning.

"Kids need so much sleep these days." Grandma licks her spoon.

Mom rolls her eyes and tells me to get our jackets. As I grab them from the hall closet, I spy Poppy's old metal lunch box. The one he brought to work every day, the heavy metal one that I watched Grandma fill with ham and cheese sandwiches, made with mustard and one crispy slice of lettuce. She used to cut them on the diagonal, wrap them up in wax paper, like they were a gift, and then she'd draw a half moon on top for Poppy. She never told me why. She said it was a special exchange between them and she did this every day. The lunch box always sat on the wooden bench by the doorway whenever he was home. That's how I knew when Poppy was home from work. Seeing it now, wedged in a dark closet, sends a tidal wave across my heart. I miss him. I miss the way he would scratch my face with his scruffy beard whenever I kissed him hello and goodbye. I reach up and grab the lunch box from the shelf with our jackets hanging over my arm.

Grandma spins around and stops talking mid-sentence when she sees the silver lunch box in my hands.

Mom says, "What on earth are you doing with that?"

"Grandma, I was wondering if, would it be possible, could I keep it?"

"Why would you want that old metal thing?" Mom asks, her hair tumbling loose from her bobby pin. "Please put it back."

"Granddaughter?" The lines in Grandma's forehead deepen as she moves closer to me.

"It just makes me think of Poppy, and I miss him and I'd like to use it for my things, that's all." I try not to let the tears prick my eyes.

"I see." Grandma pauses and exhales. "All right then, listen, you can keep it, love." She wraps her arm around my shoulder. "I think Poppy would like that. I really do."

"Hurry on, then." Mom sighs loudly and slides her long arms inside her raincoat; she tucks the loose strands of hair behind her ears. "Thanks for dinner," she says as she pushes the door open into the rain that still hasn't stopped.

"You have a good week and don't forget about next Sunday," Grandma calls to her. "And Granddaughter, you take care of that now. Thousands of notes were passed through that lunch box. Maybe even a few dirty ones too." She chuckles.

"Grandma!" I laugh, pulling on my coat.

"You've got to keep it interesting." Then she grabs both my shoulders: "I adore your new snazzy haircut." She cups my cheek with her soft, creased hand. "You're growing up so fast. A teenager, real soon."

I lunge into her arms and squeeze her waist. "I'll take care of it. I promise."

"I know. Run along but watch your step. It's slick out there."

CHAPTER 8

Mondays are hardly ever the best day of the week. But since this is the second-last one before summer holidays begin, I figure I can tolerate this less-than-average day. It's five hundred and thirty-five steps from my house to school, door to door. I used to ride my bike, at least until Mom drove over it after I forgot to put it away in the shed, like she'd asked me to a thousand times before. I haven't dared mention wanting another one again because I feel super guilty and I don't want to hear another "I told you so." Plus, I know money is always tight. She'd saved up nearly a year to buy me that bike. I reach the edge of the schoolyard and see Penny's silver station wagon.

"Wolf," she calls out to me as she springs out of the car. Her dad's been dropping her off ever since Scott died, even though they only live three blocks from the school.

Penny's wearing pink from head to toe again. Even her hair scrunchie is bubble-gum pink.

"Omigosh! Ann told me about your hair! It looks amazing. You look so stylish."

"Not bad, right?"

"Absolutely." She's nodding her head like she means it and rubs her shimmery lips together.

Wait. Is Penny wearing makeup? Since when?

I spot Brandi and Ann as they hop off their bikes and quickly lock them up across the field before running over to us.

"Your hair! YOUR HAIR!" Brandi screams. "I looove it!" she shrieks and touches it. "You're so freaking brave. I don't think I could ever cut mine so short. I would look like a total troll."

"You would not!" I say, noticing her teased-out bangs, hardened by a gallon of hairspray. I remember when we used to all dress the same. Seems like there's more that's different about us than the same these days, except for wanting to save Birchwood.

"What did your mom say about your new coiffure?" Ann asks. Her French pronunciation is as good as her English.

"Not much." I kick a rock beside my feet. I don't really feel like starting the morning off by talking about *that* conversation. Brandi steers us to a patch of grass. "Okay. So. Can we move on to something else?"

"Of course," I tell her, sinking into the lawn and letting the sun warm my bare legs.

She leans in like she's about to tell us a secret. "I know Birchwood is on everyone's minds, but are we still on for the carnival Friday night?" Brandi's unable to contain her excitement.

"I think we should still go. We can use some fun," Penny says. "Am I right?"

"I don't know." Ann pinches in her lips.

"Well," I say, "if we go Friday, then we can still get to Birchwood on Saturday, like usual. I was thinking I could try and look in my mom's office files this week to see if she has any information on new subdivisions that might link to Birchwood."

"That's a great idea," Ann says. "We can't lose sight of what's most important, even with the carnival in town." She says *carnival* like it's some sort of disease.

Everyone nods their head in agreement.

"How much are the tickets this year?" I ask, worried about my chances to have enough money to get on any rides or play games.

"Not sure," Ann answers. "To be honest, my parents are still recovering from the strike." She grabs a handful of grass.

"Yeah, same." Brandi glares down at her lap.

Penny offers Brandi a buttercup picked from the field.

"I'm just relieved it's over." Brandi tucks the tiny blossom behind her ear.

"Me too. No one thought it would last nearly nine whole months," Ann says.

Grandma Houle did. She told me so. *Mark my words*, she said, *this one's going to last for eons and screw things right up the you-know-what*.

I look at my friends and realize this is our last carnival before we start high school next fall. So many of us from the graduating class won't be together anymore, because there are five high schools to choose from. I don't even know for sure where we're all going. Neither one of us is one hundred percent decided—well, except for Ann. She's for sure going to Lockerby where the STEP program is. That's where all the brainy Smurfs go. I'm thinking about Ridgewood High, but I'm not certain. They have a really cool writer's craft program. It's such a big decision. I can't even think about that right now. Not yet. That's why every moment together feels extra special. "Okay, let's raid our piggy banks. Friday will be our new funday and then Saturday will be SOS Birchwood," I tell them. "What do you think about removing those orange flags before that? Maybe it will slow them down."

"It's a start," Ann says.

Penny sits up. "We could also strip the bands tied in the trees."

"For sure, that should delay them, at least a little," Brandi says.

"Do you guys think we should talk to someone, like an adult, about this?" Penny asks.

Ann squints in the sun. "Like who?"

She raises her shoulders. "I don't know, someone who would know about these kinds of things."

Brandi stretches and touches her toes. "What about Ms. Jeffries?"

I shield my eyes from the sun. "The geography teacher?"

"Yeah."

"I like her," Ann says.

Penny smiles. "Me too. Maybe we can ask her if she knows anything about it and we can also tell her we're worried about the land being destroyed. I think she'd definitely care about that, the way she goes on and on about the environment and stuff."

"That's a good idea," I say. "Let's talk to her."

"We'll find her after school." Brandi grabs her bag from the ground.

The bell rings and startles us all. We make our way inside and splinter off to our four different homerooms.

I say hi to Sunita from math class, but when she stares at me a second too long before waving back, I start feeling super anxious about my new haircut. Suddenly, I need to check my hair, and I'm so focused on reaching the washroom door that I almost run straight into Hari Patel.

"Hey, Wolf," he says to me. "You got a haircut."

"Oh yeah, I did." My stomach dips like I'm on a swing and going too high. I reach for my hair that's long gone. "Good weekend?"

"It was all right, I guess."

I decide I don't need to go to the washroom after all, and Hari and I continue walking in synch without talking. I begin counting my steps so I don't focus on how much I like walking next to him. Lockers are slamming on both sides of us and everyone is slow to get to homeroom. It's definitely the end of the year. No one is using their indoor voices. They're laughing out loud and hollering in the hall.

In our classes, it's been mostly movies and soccer baseball, art and free reading periods while the teachers finish up marking and filling in the report cards. We scratch one less day every morning on the chalkboard.

Denis Gervais high-fives Hari when he passes us.

"So, do you think Mr. Butterworth will be wearing his brown cardigan again today?" Hari asks me.

I grin. "I think he may actually hit a three-digit number! Brandi's been keeping track inside her math book."

"One hundred times in one year? He must *really* like that sweater," he replies. I sneak a side glance. He smiles and I smile back.

"I know," I manage to say. "I'm surprised it hasn't fallen apart!"

Hari leans in and whispers in my ear. "I heard he has five of them exactly the same hanging in his closet." He brushes my cheek with his hand, and when he does, my skin tingles and my breath gets wedged in my throat. What is happening to me?

Hari says something else but I don't hear it. I focus on my steps while my face burns from my cheeks to my forehead— even the bottoms of my ears feel hot. I can smell his shampoo drift from his wavy, black hair.

"Did you hear the carnival is coming this weekend?" he asks. I notice he's much taller than me now. When did that happen? "So, are you going? I mean, with your pack?"

"My pack?"

"You know, your wolf pack?" He chuckles. "You girls are always together, everyone knows that." He shoves his hands in his pockets.

"I guess we are." I try to keep my voice steady. "Yeah, the pack will be there. We're going on Friday." I'm smiling. I can't help it. I feel it stretch across my face like a goofy oversized elastic band.

"Good. I mean, maybe I'll see you there. And I, uh, I like your hair like that. It's different. In a good way."

"Oh. Thanks," I say, wishing I still had my long hair to disappear behind as I bolt to my seat.

What is wrong with me? Blushing and babbling and burning up in front of Hari Patel, the boy I've known since kindergarten. Hari Patel has turned Monday into a day of the week I don't recognize. Not even a little bit.

❦

The four of us are standing outside of Ms. Jeffries's class and we can see her talking to another teacher behind the glass window.

"Why am I nervous?" Brandi says. "It's not like I have detention or something."

"It's a big deal," I tell her. "It's about Birchwood."

Ms. Pelletier walks out of the room with her click-clacky high-heeled shoes and we all shuffle inside. The class is exactly like I remember it from first semester. Giant maps of the world and of Canada, provincial and territorial flags all along the back wall and a large globe sitting on her desk. How many times has that globe spun, I wonder.

"How lovely to see you all." Ms. Jeffries pushes her dark-framed glasses against her nose. "What brings you back to geography class?" She leans against her large desk.

"You know us, can't get enough of the capitals and all!" Brandi says with an awkward smile.

I clear my throat. "We're actually hoping you could help us with something," I say with as steady a voice as I can.

"Sure. I'm all ears." She crosses her legs.

Penny flashes the biggest smile ever.

I bring my feet together and straighten out. "Well, you see, we spend lots of time outside. We have a special area we like to go to."

"Outside is always the best place to be," Ms. Jeffries says.

Penny nods way too enthusiastically. "We knew you would think so."

"Well, you see . . ." I take a breath. "We were wondering if you could help us find out about some new properties being built, like who is responsible and if there's anything we can do to stop them. Because they're building it on top of our favour-ite place." I blurt out this last part really fast.

"Oh." Ms. Jeffries scrunches up her lips.

"We know how passionate you feel about preserving the land and all, from when we were in your class," Ann adds.

"I appreciate that. And I'm so proud of you for wanting to take a stand. Can you tell me where, exactly, this land is being developed?"

I look at Brandi and Penny and Ann. They all nod for me to continue. "It's on the mountain, past Kipling Park. It looks like they're developing it and the trees are already marked to be cut down."

Ms. Jeffries's face turns pale. She looks down at her feet and she's not saying anything. Anything at all.

"What's wrong?" Brandi asks her. "What is it?"

"Girls, I'm really sorry, but I won't be able to help you with this."

"No? Why not?" I ask and my heart sinks.

"Well." She takes off her glasses and pinches the skin between her eyes. She puts them back on her face. "I'm so sorry to disappoint you all. It's just, Mr. Jeffries and I, we've already submitted a deposit for one of those lots, up on the hill. We've been saving for years."

"You're going to live there? So it *is* going to be developed into a neighbourhood." My voice is shaking.

Ms. Jeffries steps away from her desk. "Yes, I'm afraid so."

"But, how?" I ask, my voice now louder than I want it to be. "Why would—? You've taught us about preserving land and caring for it. Why would you want to live there?"

"I'm really sorry. It's a done deal. We wanted to find a home that was close to both of our jobs so we could ride our bikes to work, and it's also near my aging parents, who need more support these days. It just made sense for us." She steps away and picks up a stack of notebooks along the windowsill.

My heart feels wobbly as I watch her move another pile of notebooks and then water a spider plant, pulling off the dead leaves. She doesn't say another word. Ann puts an arm around me and we all steer out of geography class for the last time.

I march down the hall, holding my breath. Once we push through the school doors, I finally exhale.

"That was a bust!" Brandi says.

Penny shakes her head, making her ponytail wag wildly from side to side. "I just can't believe it. Even Ms. Jeffries."

"I know. Talk about a shocker," I say. "And now we know for sure it's going to be a new subdivision."

"We still need to find out who is responsible," Ann says.

I scratch my forehead. "You're right. I was so upset, I forgot to even ask."

Penny tightens her ponytail. "Well, if she can't help us, then who will?"

"Let's see what I can find in my mom's office," I answer.

"And maybe we'll uncover more when we go back to the site," Ann replies. "We might be able to find some signs or the name of the construction company somewhere."

A howling, wild wind swirls around us. I have to shut my eyes so the sand doesn't sting them.

CHAPTER 9

I'm hoping to cross my mom off the list of possible people involved in the destruction of our beloved Birchwood. So after seeing Ms. Jeffries on Monday, I sneak into Mom's office and search every shelf and drawer, but I don't find a single shred of evidence that links her to the site, which is a good sign.

Then the next night, she comes home with a box, the kind that has a lid. I try to sneak back into her office while she soaks in her usual lavender bath, but the office door is locked. I didn't even know you could lock that door, so it's weird that Mom is locking it now.

On Wednesday, the girls and I go to Birchwood after school to remove the flags, but we see a bunch of workers and ATVs riding around so loudly that we freak out and decide to come back the next day.

Thankfully, on Thursday afternoon, the workers are gone. Even though we're still intimidated, we remove as many of the orange flags and plastic bands as we can. The whole time my heart is hammering, but I know we're doing the right thing. I can feel it deep inside my bones, like Grandma says. Or maybe it's the trees encouraging me as they watch us. Each flag that I stuff inside my backpack makes me feel braver, stronger. I think we're finally getting somewhere, and *doing something*, but we still need to hatch our next move.

When carnival Friday arrives, and we're making our way through the entrance, I tell the girls right away. "I still can't get into my mom's office. I'm starting to think that she's part of this."

"I can help you pick the lock," Ann says. "Seriously, the things I taught myself by having two older sisters."

"See?" Brandi takes my arm. "Just try to enjoy this night and we'll make progress tomorrow. I promise."

Between the four of us, we collected $28.50 towards the carnival.

"C'mon." Penny grabs my other arm. "Let's try to have fun tonight."

"Okay," I say, giving in and letting the jumble of carnival game music carry me forward.

"Let's check out the map." Ann flips it over in her hands, like she reads maps every single day.

Brandi reads it backwards, over her shoulder, and then rips the map from Ann's hands. "You guys!"

"What?" Penny asks on the tips of her toes, trying to catch a glimpse of the map too.

"Look!" Brandi points. "There's a psychic on site. Maybe she'll be able to see into the future!"

Ann scowls. "Not possible."

"We should try it! To see if we can learn anything, you know, about Birchwood, and maybe about, I don't know, other things like certain boys we might like or not like." Brandi lights up like a Ferris wheel.

"C'mon," Ann says, shaking her head. "That's so bogus."

"Wait a minute." I step forward. "Maybe it's worth a try. My grandma does say that some things are inexplicable, but that doesn't make them unbelievable or untrue." At least that's what she said about possible unidentified flying objects.

Ann folds her arms. "There's no way this is real."

"But what if it is?" Brandi says. "What if there's even a small chance that we can learn something and help Birchwood?"

"You know what, maybe I can ask if my mom's involved. Maybe we can actually get some answers here." And even though it seems like a wild idea, I feel like we have nothing to lose, besides of course our fun carnival money.

Ann flips her braids over her shoulders. "Don't count on it. Most of those people are quacks and just want your money."

Penny speaks up. "How much does it cost? What about the rides we want to try?" she pleads.

"We'd all have to agree," I say. "But we might not get a chance like this again. Maybe this fortune teller will be more helpful than Ms. Jeffries." Ever since our chat with her, I'd been feeling pretty discouraged. I really thought a grown-up would understand and *especially* her. Maybe this *could* help.

"Please, Ann? For Birchwood."

Ann grumbles in defeat. "Fine. Let's find the tent." She grabs the map and skims the page.

"Okay then," Penny concedes, and I'm relieved that we've all agreed.

"There it is." Ann points to a red X on the map. "Esmeralda the Magnificent." Ann rolls her eyes again.

My hope drains. "That doesn't sound promising. How serious can she be with a name like that?" I'm definitely reconsidering this.

"Well," Brandi says, "let's not judge her by her name alone." She straightens her neon green belt and starts in the direction of Esmeralda's tent.

The strident sounds of the carnival swirl around us as we make our way through the crowds, finally arriving at the quieter booths, the ones closer to the end of the parking lot. It's more isolated and feels a little creepy with fewer people walking around.

"There it is." I point to the blinking, bright sign: *Esmeralda the Magnificent*.

We gingerly approach the striped tent and I notice another sign with small print.

This reading is final. Once you enter the tent and payment is made, there is no refund, no matter what. Esmeralda the Magnificent will not be held responsible for any choices that are made due to the information passed from her to the paying client. The tarot is a powerful tool used to tell fortunes. It is not a game. Visitors should consider themselves warned.

Penny pulls on her blond braid, the tip bleached white from the sun. "I'm not sure about this anymore."

"We're all in this together," I say to her, trying to quiet her fears, and mine too.

Brandi turns to face us. "C'mon people, we *need* help figuring out how to save Birchwood," she says.

Ann nods firmly.

"Well, okay," Penny whispers. I grab her hand and give a small squeeze.

"All in?" I ask, scanning their faces.

"All in." They nod their heads up and down. I suck in another breath and push aside the hefty red curtain. A man ambles out like a zombie, looking totally spooked. Penny claws her fingernails into my skin. I drag her with me and we creep our way in together, arms linked like a chain.

"Step forward," a hoarse voice says. "Let me look at you."

We shuffle ahead, inching ourselves into her candlelit view. It smells like she's burning something, a strong perfume, and then I spot the black swirling triangle on a plate by her hands, its smoke spiralling through the top of the tent.

"Now I see you all," she says. "And your money. Show me your money, girls."

Ann fans the money out onto the table: one ten, one five, two twos and a one-dollar bill.

"Wonderful."

"Can we get a reading together?" I ask. Esmeralda doesn't look like anyone I've ever seen before. She's wearing a poufy purple satin robe with large pink shoulders and a matching purple head wrap. I can't see any of her hair. I don't even know if she has any. But her skin is as white as porcelain and you can see her blue veins bleeding through, like ink staining a white page.

"Each reading is ten minutes. That's all I can offer for twenty dollars, even if you have more than one person in the room."

"That's plenty," Ann answers.

"Wonderful." She grins an extra-wide smile. "All right, let's get started, shall we? Who'd like to shuffle the deck of cards for the group?" she says, picking it up.

"I vote Wolf," Brandi says.

"Me too," Penny adds.

"Fine then, Wolf, the girl with the interesting name. Your friends vote you the shuffler of destinies."

I stare at the thick deck and my stomach dips again. I've only ever seen these at Grandma's friend Bonnie's house. She has a whole collection of these cards with different art and animals printed on them that she stores in a tall glass case.

"You should sit down to do this. It will be easier. The others can stand behind you. Well, go on then." She slides the pile of cards across the table.

I pull out the metal chair, and as I sit down, I realize that Esmeralda is extremely tall, even though she's sitting down. And now that I'm closer to her, I also realize that her breath smells worse than Mr. Butterworth's constant coffee breath. I hold my breath and pick up the cards.

"Now shuffle until you feel called to stop."

I exhale and pick up the deck.

"While she's doing this, the rest of you should be hushing your minds. You can ask three questions. Understood?"

"Yes," Ann says.

"Wonderful."

My heart races as I shuffle the ginormous red cards with golden sides. They have a cloaked woman standing beside a lion and a full moon hanging above them printed on the back side. You can tell the cards have been used for almost a million years because the edges are so frayed. I stop when I think I have shuffled long enough. No one utters a single word.

"Before we proceed, I need to ensure that you read the conditions outside of the tent. Once I flip the first card"—she points her extra-long finger towards us—"absolutely no refunds no matter what. Clear?"

I swear everyone can hear my heart booming in my chest.

"All right then, let's proceed. Please cut the deck in three stacks."

I do what she tells me and wait for the answers we seek.

I can feel the girls sway behind me, their searing breath on the back of my neck.

"What's the question?" Esmeralda asks us.

"I, uh, well . . ." Brandi hesitates.

"Speak up. And remember, the question cannot be answered by a yes or no."

"How can we help save Birchwood?" Ann blurts out. I turn to look at her and she raises her shoulders questioningly at me. I nod for her to know that it was a good first question.

"Wonderful," Esmeralda says. "Please choose a card from the first deck."

I follow her instruction, and she takes the card from my hands and flips it over: "THE TOWER CARD," she announces. "This card signifies change. Change is imminent and trying to prevent it could lead to disaster. It also represents looming chaos and destruction with a warning to surrender to this upheaval that's about to happen." She taps the edge of the card on the table. "Life is about creating and destroying. It's a messy cycle, but what can I say? It's the way it is."

Penny shrieks and I grip the sides of the chair.

"Now listen," Esmeralda says, with her voice extra gruff, all ten flaming fingernails in the air, "you scream like that again and you're out! I won't have you frightening the people next in line."

My mind flashes to the guy who walked out before us. I wonder what card he got?

"But what does that mean?" Brandi's voice quivers. "What should we worry about *the most* right now?"

"Is that your second question?"

Brandi quickly nods her head.

"Okay, then. Let's see what the cards say. Wolf, please choose a card from the second deck."

I fan the cards out and carefully choose one. Esmeralda flips over the card: "THE DEATH CARD."

A skeleton stands hunched over holding a scythe.

Penny slaps both hands against her mouth. I scream on the inside and dig my fingernails into the surface of the wooden table.

Esmeralda bends her giraffe neck forward to look Penny in the eyes. "Child, I know this card may seem alarming, but it doesn't always mean what you think it means. What is your name, girl?"

"Penny."

"Penny, lucky Penny, this card can represent an ending and not a death," she speaks, slowly now. "Sometimes endings must happen in order for a new beginning to be born. Like winter must happen in order for summer to return. It's not a bad thing. It's a necessary thing. Do you understand this?"

I crane my neck to see Penny.

"Uh-huh." Penny wipes tears from her eyes. I'm certain the death Penny is thinking of is her brother's.

We all look at each other. Our eyes are as wide as saucers. These are not the kinds of answers we were looking for.

Esmeralda checks her watch. "What is your third and last question?"

I just sit there, blinking in the dark, opening and closing my eyes.

"Time is ticking, ladies."

Though I'm not sure any of us are ready, a question comes to me and I blurt it out.

"Will we be friends forever?" I know it's a yes or no question but it's all I could think of. She nods her head, and so I reach for a third card in the third pack and my hand is visibly shaking. I slide it across the table to her. Esmeralda takes it and flips it over slowly . . . "THE TEN OF SWORDS." Ten swords piercing through a man's back and blood soaking his clothes.

"Now . . ." Esmerelda softens her voice. "This card does signify an inevitable ending, a type of loss that is not desired, but one that must happen in order for you to grow and evolve into your fullest potential. It is always purposeful, but often painful. So." She curls in her magenta-painted lips and pauses. "Sorry, but I sense this quartet will be over by the end of the summer. Furthermore"—she leans forward with her nose nearly touching mine—"before this denouement, a friend in this room will cause one of you to suffer a broken heart."

Gasps tear through the small candlelit tent; our shock waves fill every speck of breathing space. I slowly rise from the chair and stand beside my friends.

"Oh, girls!" she calls. "One last tidbit. A bonus message, if you will."

I hold my breath and wait wistfully, swaying slightly front to back on my toes.

"Lucky little Penny," she says, "your brother Scott is watching over you."

Penny's knees give out and I lean over to support her. Brandi and Ann are standing like frozen statues as the velvet curtain is ripped open.

How on earth did she know Scott's name?

Esmeralda is the real deal. This is what we were hoping for, right?

We step out into the madness of lights and sounds. The screams of the carnival whip around us. I feel like I'm spiralling, but my feet are planted in place, my friendship pins are still fastened to my shoes. Brandi grabs my arm and our eyes meet for a split second. She looks terrified. Penny looks like she's going to bawl at any moment and Ann is scrubbing her glasses repeatedly with the bottom of her peach shirt.

"I don't buy it," Brandi says.

"But what about Scott? How could she know about him?" I say.

"Lucky guess," Brandi replies, but she sounds unsure.

Penny says, "That's a pretty lucky guess. I believe her."

"If she's a true psychic, then why doesn't she work for the police to help find missing people or something? Why work at a carnival? I think it's bull chicken." Brandi crosses her arms.

"What do you think, Ann?" Penny asks.

Ann's shaking her head. "How could she know his name? How?" She keeps staring off into the distance. We sit down on the corner of a cement parking curb to catch our breath, to process what we heard in there. It's hard to piece it all together. All I know right now is that none of it sounded good.

In the distance, I think I hear my name being called. When I look up, I see Hari Patel walking towards us, with his older brother and Denis Gervais, Brandi's big crush.

"I thought it was the legendary wolf pack," Hari says when he reaches me, his face full of light.

I try to muster a smile but it's hard. I can't stop thinking about what Esmeralda said about our group's friendship being over by the end of this summer. I stare at my feet again. Kick dirt. A cloud settles over my shoes.

"You girls try any rides yet?" Denis Gervais asks.

"Not yet," Ann says. "We kind of just got here." She straightens her glasses on her nose.

"Well, why don't we try the Zipper?" he offers. "I have two arm-lengths of tickets to use up before tonight's late ice time. You gotta love triple-A hockey team perks."

For a minute, we all exchange glances. I can tell no one is quite sure how to shake off what happened in Esmeralda's tent. But then Brandi straightens up. "Okay," she answers, jostling her neon bracelets up her arm. And the rest of us nod and get up too. As a group, we flock towards the blinking lights and booming music.

An hour later, my stomach is churning from too many rides and watching Brandi flirt with Denis Gervais, non-stop. We watch the boys lose a couple of games, and then we use our leftover change to buy cotton candy. We park ourselves by the carousel, but I'm sitting to the side, away from Hari, because I'm afraid I might hurl and the last thing I want to do is make this night even worse by blowing pink chunks in front of him. Thankfully, the boys leave as soon as they inhale their cotton candy. I fling the rest of my sweet pink cloud in the garbage. My stomach is still a total disaster. Think hurricane combined with a tornado.

We haven't had a chance to say much to each other about the reading from Esmeralda the Magnificent.

We take a shortcut through the train tracks to get home and everyone is still being really quiet. "Hey, so, should we talk about what happened?" I say into the dark. The stars are barely visible with the carnival flashing in the distance.

"I don't know, I just want to forget about it," Penny says.

I jump on the metal rail, trying to balance both feet. The night air is helping calm my stomach, but I can still smell the incense on my clothes.

"I think we should discuss it," Ann pipes in. "It was pretty intense."

Brandi picks up her pace. "I'm with Penny. I'd rather not."

This doesn't happen often—two of us feeling differently than the other two. Almost never. Especially about the big things. The most important things. "Why don't we sleep on it," I say.

"Fine. Usual place and time tomorrow?" Ann asks.

Brandi pitches a rock as far as she can.

Silence still surges, but everyone offers a curt nod.

The summer breeze blows through the leaves as we get to our splitting-off point. Ann cuts through a trail, while Brandi and Penny take the road, on opposite sides.

I sprint as fast as I can, without touching the tracks, counting my steps on each wooden slab, feeling the night press down on me and totally regretting our decision to meet Esmeralda the Magnificent. I wanted to learn how to save Birchwood, and now I feel like there are even more things I need to save.

CHAPTER 10

Grandma says the seasons remind us that nothing stays the same, even though we may want that more than anything. No matter how fast or how slow you want the days to go, the seasons always end and start again. You only have to look at the trees to see this. They are constantly changing, yet they still grow up and out.

Today is a day of change. It's Saturday, June 21, which means it's officially the first day of summer. Grandma prefers to call this day Summer Solstice. She says it's one of the most important days of the year, especially for Indigenous People. It's a time of great celebration to give thanks to the sun for all of the ways it helps us grow our food and keeps us warm. Grandma also says it's a great day to start anew.

"Good morning," Mom greets me as I eagerly come downstairs. Her long, dark hair is loose and spills over her shoulder. "Up early this morning?"

"Yup! First day of summer, just trying to make the most of it," I say. "Longest day of the year, you know. What does Grandma always say? *Carpe diem!*" I chug the glass of cold orange juice she hands to me and pull out a chair.

"I'm happy to hear you say that because we're marking *this* special Saturday with a day on a boat!" she announces with a strange drum-roll on the counter. What is up with my mom lately?

"A boat? What about your open houses?" Why is she spending another weekend not working?

"Not today," Mom shoots back, like she has a master plan up her sleeve.

"Whose boat? I have plans with my—"

"Wolf, listen. I want you to meet my friend, my friend Roger," she says, smoothing down her flower-patterned skirt.

"Roger who?" I grab a piece of toast from a plate. I only know two Rogers. One is our neighbour, Roger Charbonneau who drove a school bus for almost fifty years and he's in his seventies. There's only one other Roger. I wrinkle my nose. "Not Roger Carling from Carling King Construction?"

Mom's lips curve into a smile. "He's a very nice man. I've actually known him since high school and we've been working together for years now. We make a pretty good team."

Is she blushing?

"We share lots in common and—"

I feel my forehead rumple. Wait, did she say she's been working with him? My mind races back to the new box of files she brought home, and her locked office door. These couldn't be related, could they?

"I have plans with my friends," I say firmly. If I stay home, I can sneak into her office and then meet up with the pack. Besides, we still have so much to discuss since Esmeralda's shocking reading last night. "Can I just stay home? Please?"

"This is important to me. Roger would like to meet you and I think it's time."

Mom and I lock eyes and I feel myself slouch deeper into the upholstered chair. I can't believe my luck. Roger Carling? Why does it have to be that Roger, out of all the Rogers in the entire world? How am I going to get through this? Think, Wolf, think. And then, an idea pops into my head. "Well, okay fine. I'll go with you on the boat, but then could I have a sleepover tonight? It is my birthday next week, after all."

She looks at me, somewhat relieved. "Fine," she replies, without any delay.

"Really?"

"Don't make me change my mind. Hurry up and go get ready. You'll need to wear layers. It might get cold on the water." She wipes the counter and rinses out my glass.

"Okay, thanks." I spring to my feet.

"I really hope you'll give him a chance." Mom's eyelids open and close, gently, like butterfly wings. "He's been very kind to me."

I sigh. "I will, Mom. I'll try," I say, even though this feels like it might be really hard.

"Thanks, honey. I appreciate that. Now go put your bathing suit on under your clothes. We'll be leaving soon."

Before we leave for the day, I call Ann from the phone in Mom's room, for a little privacy.

"Ann, it's Wolf. I don't have much time to talk. Long story. But, I was hoping you could call the girls for me and invite them to sleep over at my place tonight."

"Wow! Tonight?"

"Yeah. Another super 'Sudbury Saturday Night.' Can you make it?"

"I hope so. I'll ask."

"Okay, great. Tell everyone to be here at like seven p.m. Sorry, I have to go. I'll fill you in later. Promise."

"Okay."

"Tonight," I say and hang up the phone.

We're waiting in the driveway, standing by our single maple tree, the three of us shoulder to shoulder to trunk. Mom flashes me an awkward king-size smile and reaches for my cheek. "Be extra nice, okay?" she says. I turn my head away and focus on the ants by my feet.

I should have suspected Mom was seeing somebody because for the past few weeks, she's been wearing new nail polish, perfume and fancy high-heeled shoes, the kind that show your toes. Classic signs. But now that it's confirmed, it feels weird.

A noise rips through the clear sky. The whirring of nearby lawn mowers gets buried by a rumbling coming up the road. Mom squeezes my arm. I stretch my neck to see the source of the racket: it's a Trans Am, machismo red with shiny rims. It's you-know-who pulling up; his dark hair is slicked back and he's wearing aviator glasses.

"Isn't his car a beauty?"

Since when does she care about cars?

"Well, well, well, look what we got here." Roger rolls down his window. "Don't you two look pur-dy." He tips his tinted sunglasses away from his face, exposing his bushy eyebrows.

"Oh, Roger, quit it," Mom says in a voice I've never heard before. He doesn't get out of the car. Mom opens the door on our side and pulls the seat forward so I can climb into the back seat. After she sits in the front, she leans in next to Roger and he kisses her cheek. I look away. I don't know how to deal with all of this.

"This here is Wolf, my big girl," Mom says, turning around to pat my knee several times—too many times—with her palm.

He eyeballs me through his rear-view mirror. "An honour to meet you, Wolf." He tips his head again. "Your pretty mom has told me you're a quite a gal."

"All good things, Wolf. I promise." She beams at Roger.

What is happening to my mom? I've heard opposites attract, but Mom reads Charlotte Brontë, Virginia Woolf and Jane Austen. She listens to classical music. CBC radio. She's never been into boats, cars or moustaches! I look out the window and count the blackbirds sitting on the wire. For some reason I think about Hari. Are we similar or different? I know he likes nature, like me, because he goes camping and fishing. He's also humble and shy, likes animals, and he's really good at math, basketball and—. Wait. What is happening to me? I think my fever is spreading again.

"You don't bite, do you?" Roger asks me as I buckle up.

"Pardon me?" I try to remain polite, squeeze my knees together.

He chuckles. "I mean, you know, with your wolf teeth?"

"Oh, Roger, quit it." Mom nudges his shoulder, and her hand lingers as she smooths his hair behind his large ear.

I groan softly. "Funny one," I say and howl loudly on the inside.

"All right, pretty ladies, let Roger get you out of here and onto the open water. It's going to be a ridiculously hot, hot day!" He backs onto the road and steps on the accelerator. I bend from side to side in the back seat while the seatbelt cinches my waist, watching Mom giggle and scratch the back of Roger's neck with her long, painted nails.

Could this be the chaos Esmeralda was talking about when we pulled the Tower card? This certainly is a change I didn't expect, and it feels like it's flipping my world upside down.

Roger drives like a cowboy, at least that's what Grandma Houle would say. Turning hard around the corners. Showing off because he's got nothing to show for. I grip the leather seat to stop my body from crashing into the door and notice some papers shuffling under my feet. There's a Carling King Construction logo stamped on a folder with the words *Northwood Heights, Coming Soon* printed across it. My insides turn. If my mom and Roger are a team, what exactly have they been working on?

CHAPTER 11

It takes almost twenty minutes to drive to the boat launch at Ramsey Lake, which feels more like an hour in the back seat of this car. When we finally arrive, we have to wait another five minutes for Roger to smoke a cigarette and unload the coolers packed with drinks and food before we proceed to the marina where his boat is kept. I spot his boat in a split second: bright red with a white interior. *Nickel City King* is painted across it.

After we climb into the speedboat, he takes us to the centre of the lake, but only after we circle around a few times at ridiculously high speeds. I'm feeling motion sick, so I try to focus on a small island I see in the distance. The Tree People are leaning into each other like they are huddling from the wind. Finally, I hear the motor cut out and watch Roger throw in the anchor. Mom wastes no time. She pulls her long mane into an elastic band and snaps a quick bun behind her head. "I'm going in! Anyone else?"

"No thanks," I answer. "The lake's all yours." I squint in the sun, my bottom sticking to the vinyl seat. I should have worn pants.

"I'll watch your girl, here." Roger winks at me.

Mom pulls off her long skirt and blouse and uncovers her bathing suit underneath, the striped black-and-white one. She folds her clothes neatly into a pile and leaves them on her seat. She then dives in like a pro swimmer. No splash whatsoever. I still have to pinch my nose so I don't choke on water when I jump in.

"So, what do you think, Wolf?" Roger asks, watching my mom swim away.

"About what?" I reply, counting my mom's front strokes.

He gets up from the driver's seat and comes closer, to the bench directly across from me. "You having a good time? On the boat, I mean." His nicotine breath wafts in my face. I wrap my hands around my stomach.

"Your mom told me your Poppy used to take you fishing on his boat. I like to fish, too."

He knows about Poppy? "I'm not that into fishing these days," I say.

"Of course. You're pretty much a teenager now." He lifts his sunglasses, plops them on top of his head and combs his moustache down with his finger and thumb.

"Yeah. Something like that."

"Well, me and your mom are getting along real well, and it'd be good for us to get along, too."

I swallow hard.

"Your mom's told me a lot about you and what it's been like, without a dad around."

I cross and uncross my ankles. I don't know how I feel about him knowing personal stuff about me, about us and *our* family. I realize now what a terrible idea it was to agree to come here, on this boat. There's nowhere to go. I'm stuck here.

Roger looks down at his sandals. "I'm not really used to girls," he says, with a shaky voice, "but I'm a—, I'm a willing to try real hard for us to become pals."

I think he might be blushing but I can't be sure with this heat. And for some reason, something in me softens. I want to tell him that it's possible, that maybe I can perhaps not despise this dating situation, someday. That I want my mom to be happy, that maybe we could even go fishing together in the future because I really do miss that pure excitement of a fish tugging on my line. I also miss Poppy. A lot. But those words don't surface. Instead, I grip the sides of my seat and dig my heels into the waterproof carpet.

"What kind of construction do you do?" I ask him. Because this feels important.

"Construction? Well, I build homes for Sudbury's development initiatives. Why?" he asks. I can tell I've caught him off guard.

"I'm just curious. I wasn't sure if you built bridges, repaired roads or—"

"Nope. I build new neighbourhoods and I love doing it."

"Oh. I was afraid of that."

His face scrunches. "And why's that?"

"Well . . ." I take an extra-long breath. "I guess you can say we have different philosophical beliefs."

"What the hairy canary does that mean?" he asks, tilting his head.

"You're on the other side of things. Like my mom."

I can't help myself. My words spill out like gumballs from the machine at the A&P. Bluegreenredorangeyellowpurple. "It means we disagree on major issues. Critical ones." I feel my forehead beading with sweat. I wipe it with the back of my hand.

He looks amused. "Really, like what?"

The hot sun beats down on the back of my neck. I wish I were a bird so I could take off from this boat. But I can't, so my words keep somersaulting into the air. "You destroy animal homes. Wreck the environment. You make money by killing forests."

The lines on his forehead darken, like a brazen mini-storm on a hot summer day. "I see." He wipes his brow. "Your mom told me you were touchy about trees." His chin rises to where she's floating on her back, twenty feet away.

"I'm not touchy. I just really care about other living things. I think we all should." The boat rocks back and forth as the waves from another boat reach us.

"Okay, listen. Hear me out. I build homes for people. For families. I'm a hard-working man trying to do honest work." He shows me his open hands, like he has nothing to hide. "Don't you think people deserve to live in nice homes?"

"How's it going up there?" Mom hollers from the water. "I'm going to swim out a bit farther," she says, her hair pasted flat against her head.

"Take your time, my little mermaid," he answers, waving her on. He turns back to me, like a cloud covering the sun.

"Me and your mom have plans for this town. We want to make it beautiful again, like it was long before the mining started polluting everything. We don't want to be known as the ugly town anymore. Your mom and I want to help grow this city. Develop it. We're a really good team. I hope to Saturn you can see that."

I unfold my arms and blink into the blinding sun.

"I meant it when I said I wanted us to get along. I really care about your mom. I hope you'll let me care about you too, even if we have different philosophical beliefs and all."

He sounds sincere, but I don't respond. This is a lot to take in. Instead, I sit and sulk with my skin cooking in the high sun while Roger cranks music from the boat speakers. I look out onto the water and spot Mom's tiny head, bobbing back towards us. I consider jumping in with all of my clothes on, just to get away from him and his so-called music. But I'm not so sure I want to be with my mom right now, either.

"That was so refreshing," Mom says when she finally climbs back into the boat. "You should have brought your bathing suit, Wolf."

"Next time," Roger says, handing her a large towel and grinning at her ear to ear.

"Thank you for today," Mom tells me, as we amble up the driveway. Roger honks his horn and his tires squeal when he turns the corner. She waves at his disappearing car with level-ten enthusiasm.

"It means a lot to me that you were with us today," she says as we make our way inside.

"Sure thing."

"Do you like him?"

"Well—"

"I know it might be weird for you, at first, to have a man around. It's always been just you and me. I'm only asking you to give him a chance."

"He did feed the ducks," I manage to say. Even though you aren't supposed to feed the ducks, I hold back.

"He's really wonderful. You'll see." Guilt rushes to my stomach, hitches itself to my heart and pulls. I sink into her body and lean my head against her chest. It's been years since I've seen Mom this happy. "Let's get ready for that sleepover I promised you," she says after squeezing me real hard and planting a kiss on my head.

"Thanks," I say. I'm ready to switch gears too.

CHAPTER 12

We don't have much time to prepare, but Mom drives to the corner store to grab the necessities: Doritos and Twizzlers and, of course, Dr Pepper. She also says she'll make homemade pizzas.

A short while later, my room looks like an all-girls school has invaded it. The last time the whole gang slept over was at least two birthdays ago. Regular sleepovers usually happen at Penny's place (best snacks) or Brandi's (most privacy—basement bedroom) so it feels really special that everyone is here.

I decide it's a good time for us to talk about what happened yesterday. "I'm so glad you're all here!" I say. "We really need to stick together. Now, more than ever."

Ann leans against my bed and stretches her long legs onto the floor. "You're right, we have to band together for the sake of Birchwood and our friendship."

"No matter what," Brandi says. "I'm sorry I was such a drama queen last night. I was just really freaked out."

"It was pretty freaky," I say.

"So, should we talk about Esmeralda? About, you know, *all* the things she said?"

I know what Brandi's referring to—a future betrayal and our friendships coming to an end. It just doesn't seem possible right now, sitting here together, fully determined to save Birchwood. I look at Ann and she looks away.

"Why don't we just stay focused on our mission," I answer, not wanting any more potential drama after today's already strange events. Still, I should check in on Penny.

"How about you?" I put a hand on her shoulder. "How are you doing since the reading?"

"Well, at first I was truly terrified, but now, it's kinda nice, comforting even, to know Scott is somewhere, still, watching over me."

"I'm glad." I give her a one-arm hug.

Brandi gives her a one-arm hug too. Then she says, "So what's the plan for tonight, party people?"

"Shhh . . . I was thinking we'd go up to the mountain to see if removing those orange flags slowed down any of their progress," I whisper. "We might also find more clues about who's responsible, which company, I mean."

"Like construction signs?" Ann asks.

"Exactly. After that, we can come back and pick the lock to my mom's office, like you mentioned."

Ann smiles a delighted smile. "I brought my tools."

"Good. Because I'm really starting to suspect that my mom is involved."

"Really?" Brandi asks a little too loud.

"Yes," I whisper back. "You guys, she's dating Roger from Carling King Construction and they're working together on something. I had to spend the whole day with them on his boat, but before that, I saw a file in his car with *Northwood Heights, Coming Soon* printed across it."

"No way! That could definitely be linked to Birchwood," Ann says.

"I know," I answer, feeling the worry swell in my stomach again.

"They're dating?" Brandi says, like she can't believe it herself.

"Yeah."

"What if she catches us?" Penny says softly. "In her office, I mean."

"She won't. We just can't let that happen," I tell her.

A rapid knock at the door makes us all jump and look up.

Mom walks in holding something wrapped. "I was going to wait to give you this on your *actual* birthday, but I think you'll enjoy it more tonight." She hands me a medium-sized box, as long as a shoebox but more narrow.

"Is it what I think it is? Is it, Mom?" I quickly unwrap it.

"Happy almost thirteenth birthday, Wolf." She bends down and kisses my cheek. "A teenager!"

"My very own phone!" I squeal and everyone huddles in close. "Thank you so much. I can't believe you bought me one for my room!" My happiness meter is off the charts right now.

"Have fun now, girls, and don't get too carried away, okay? I'll call you down once the pizza is ready."

I pull the phone out of the box.

"It's so cool!" Ann says.

Brandi leans in super close. "Do the numbers glow in the dark? I wish my mom would buy me one of those."

"They do! It's the one from Woolworth's I was gawking at for months."

"Mint green!" Penny exclaims.

Brandi says, "Oh wow, it's the best!"

"Plug it in!" Penny grabs the cord. "Who should we call first?"

"Denis Gervais!" Brandi shouts.

And for some reason, this super unsurprising, totally predictable response makes me roll over on my back and laugh until my belly hurts so much I seriously cannot even breathe. One by one, they all start to laugh too: Brandi, Penny and even Ann. Once we collect ourselves, Ann quickly delegates.

"Wolf, get the phone book."

"He lives on Danforth," Brandi chirps.

"Okay, stalker." I push her leg with my foot.

"I know things," she replies, her eyes sparkling.

"Wait. Who's going to talk?" Ann asks.

"Not me." Brandi curls her feet in under her. "It's your phone, you should use it first, Wolf."

"Fine." I really don't feel like talking to Denis, but I do want to try out my phone, and all my friends are already here, so I dial the numbers. Each number makes the sweetest sound I've ever heard. I hold the receiver and it rings three times before I anxiously say, "Hello. Is Denis there, please?"

"It's me, Denis. It's Denis," he says. I cover my mouth with my hand.

"Hello? He-llo? Who is this?" he's saying on the other end.

I'm clasping the receiver in the air and we can't hold it in anymore and we laugh so hard and I don't push the hang-up button until after Brandi yells, "WOLF, HANG UP!"

"Oh my god! I'm so humiliated. Now he knows it was *me*! Seriously! Why did you yell out my name?"

Brandi pulls on my arm. "I didn't mean to! I'm sorry!" She groans. "You guys, we have to call back." Her eyes are huge, like a fly.

"No way! I'm not calling him back."

"I will," Penny says.

"You will?" We ask, each with a confused look our face. Penny flips her shoulder-length hair.

"It's just a phone call, right?"

Brandi bites down on her lower lip and thinks. "Okay, do it." She grabs the phone from my hands and puts it in Penny's lap. She hits the redial number without hesitating, like calling him is a super-normal, everyday thing.

"Hi, Denis. It's Penny. Sorry for hanging up on you. Wolf is here, and Brandi and Ann too." Brandi covers her face with her hands. "What are we doing? Well, we're having a sleepover at Wolf's, and then"—Penny continues like she's talking to any of us. She's cool. Not shy. Who is this person?—"we're heading to the woods." Shrieks erupt across the room. Penny slaps her hand against her mouth and drops the phone in Brandi's lap and Brandi shakes her head so violently that Ann takes the receiver.

"Denis, Ann here. What are *you* doing tonight?" She asks like a boss. "Uh-huh, okay. Let me check."

Ann shields the bottom of the phone receiver with her palm and whispers, "He wants to know if he and Hari and Binks can meet us later? At the school?"

Brandi nods her head eagerly.

My stomach does a sudden backflip. Hari? "Um. Fine. Okay," I mutter and tuck a short strand of hair behind my ear. "But not the woods," I whisper back. "We cannot show them Birchwood. Remember how long it took for that group from Nesbitt Public to stop coming around?" And as I picture meeting up with Hari tonight, on the Summer Solstice, of all nights, my body starts buzzing again, like that time we spoke in the hall.

Ann flips a thumbs-up, checks her watch and says into the phone, "We'll meet you at the school in an hour."

CHAPTER 13

We gobble up our pizza and decide to try to find Ms. Barry in the phone book, but we totally do not succeed. She's so old school she probably doesn't even own a phone. We crank call half a dozen more teachers and classmates, and then we hatch out our plan.

"Okay, let's confirm the details for tonight," I say. "After we meet with the boys, let's swing by Birchwood to make sure there haven't been any other developments."

"It's priority. We'll also look for more clues," Ann says.

"Exactly. And, right after that, we'll try to get into my mom's office to look through that box. We either rule her out or we find out the truth." I swallow hard. "We need to stay dedicated to what's most important, no matter what boys we see tonight."

"I agree," Ann says. "We can't lose focus now. Does your mom keep her desk or file cabinet locked too?"

"Not usually. I was thinking the two of us can look for evidence and Brandi and Penny could stand guard, in case she wakes up."

"I'm an expert at that," Brandi says. "I've been practising my whole life with my own sister. I am total spy material."

Penny says, "I can pretend I had a nightmare or something like that to buy you some time. I can really bring the waterworks on when I need them."

"Perfect." I push up my sleeves. "Solid plan."

I check in on Mom before we leave. Her favourite TV show is on, *The Golden Girls*, but she's already sleeping heavily—thanks to all things lavender. Plus, with the fresh air she had from her best day on the boat, she'll be snoozing for the night.

We sneak out the back sliding door because Penny's too afraid to jump from my bedroom window. We run down the road in a straight line until we turn the corner onto Gemmell Street, where we finally exhale.

Being out at night with no one on the streets, except for a random stray cat, feels pretty special. I wish I could press pause and stay here with my friends for eternity, at this very moment, on this first night of summer, on my almost birthday. I can't imagine us not being friends forever. I feel certain that Esmeralda got that one completely wrong. At least, I really, really hope she did.

I'm taking the lead while Ann follows close behind. Penny is at the very end, and of course, Brandi is zigzagging between us all. I smile at the Tree People standing guard, one tree planted in every front yard, with their leaves whirling in the warm breeze, as if they're waving at us. *Hello, beautiful maples and pines*, I say to them, without words.

"My parents will kill me if they find out we snuck away after dark," Penny says.

"Totally." Brandi skips beside her. "That's why we can't get caught."

"So far, so good." I look behind me, stretching my ears for any footsteps in the distance.

Ann whispers, "Let's keep it down until we get to the school."

Once we reach the path that leads to Rockwood Public, Brandi starts to bounce on the tips of her feet. She's more jittery than usual.

"I hope you're not getting all boy crazy on us, Brandi. Once that happens, there's no getting you back. I've seen it with both of my sisters," Ann says.

"You're such a square," Brandi replies in a lighthearted way, walking backwards so she can talk to us.

"I am not. I just find boys really immature."

"Not all of them are." Penny snickers. "Especially the cute ones," she adds, laughing now. "Am I right?"

"I knew you were my favourite, Penny," says Brandi.

They high-five and I marvel at how comfortable they are

talking about this stuff. I feel grateful Ann seems as uncomfortable about it as I am.

"So, Wolf, I've noticed Hari sure likes talking to you," Brandi comments.

"Yeah, he's cute too," Penny says.

"He's nice, okay, but we have to keep our wits about us. For Birchwood." *I* have to keep my wits in check, most of all. I exhale.

"Didn't you tell me once that Summer Solstice encourages love connections? That your grandma said it was an enchanted night?" Brandi asks.

My stomach does a backflip. She's right. Grandma Houle did tell me that. And suddenly I'm not sure going to see the boys is the best idea. "Let's not get off track. We've got to make the most of this night together, for Birchwood." Especially after all of the Esmeralda stuff.

"We'll see." She grabs Penny's hand and takes off running for the school, leaving Ann and me in their shadows.

Ann shakes her head. "Those two are hopeless."

I exhale again. Slowly. Trying to calm the squall gaining strength in my belly.

We proceed to the back of the school, where we hang out at recess, and I see them: Hari, Denis and Binks. They're throwing rocks at each other and dodging them.

"Real mature," Ann says.

Binks is his last name; his first name is Jonathan. But he looks like a Justin. That's because all Justins look like troublemakers in my book. He's been in our class since grade six.

Hari drops the rock he was holding when he spots me and then shuffles awkwardly over to us.

"I thought for sure you girls would've chickened out," Denis says.

"Us?" Brandi flips her hair. "You have no idea." She starts to giggle when Denis gets closer.

"We're not afraid," Penny chirps.

"Hey, Penny, is that you? You look different in the dark," Denis says. "I'm glad you called me back."

Binks kicks a rock like a hacky sack. "Yeah, ever since you were paired up for dance in gym class last year—"

"Shut up, Binks." Denis looks annoyed.

"Well, it's true, doofus."

Ann and I swing our heads and look at Brandi, who is wincing under the moonbeam. She's unable to hide her disappointment at the fact that he's talking to Penny, staring at Penny, and most likely, probably, likes Penny.

"Well, I didn't call back for me." Penny says quickly, her eyes darting from him to Brandi. "I called for—"

"Me!" I interrupt. "I, um . . . hadn't meant to hang up when I called you on my new phone. How come you don't have hockey tonight?"

"Weekend off."

"I guess even Gretzky gets the night off once in a while," Ann says.

"Hilarious," he replies.

Brandi is gaping at the ground. I'm not sure how to fix this.

"So, what should we do?" Binks asks, and it sounds like he's up to trouble.

I focus on the school, on the three spotlights beaming against the brick wall. It looks weird at night with so many dark, shadowed corners. I feel like leaving and heading straight to Birchwood. Why did we decide to do this? I glance over at Hari and he's looking back at me. My stomach flip-flops. I press my hands against it discreetly.

"What about Truth or Dare?" Binks says. He lobs a rock into the tree line.

"No way," Ann shoots back faster than a speeding bullet.

"What, you scared?"

"Me? Ha! Just not interested."

"Nerd alert," he says, like he's proud of himself.

Ann quickly crosses and uncrosses her arms. "Fine. I'll play. But it's my turn first. Hari," she says, "truth or dare?"

Truth. Truth. Truth. Please let it be truth. I suck in my breath.

"Truth," he answers.

Thank god.

"Do you like somebody here? *Like* like," she asks, "you know, more than a friend?"

I try to look as normal as possible. I can't believe Ann just asked him that like it's a routine question.

"Maybe," he answers, not letting his eyes divulge anything.

"That's not an answer."

"Fine then. Yes." He shoves his hands in his pockets.

I freeze and I realize I'm trying not to smile. But then I

realize that he could mean anyone. Could he like Penny? Or Brandi? Ann?

"Boring!" Binks shouts. "No more Truth or Dare. Dares only," he says.

"Fine with me." Hari flips his hair off his face. "Ann, I dare you to kiss Binks."

She pauses for three whole seconds and then, to my complete surprise, she marches straight up to him.

"Cheek only and close your eyes," she says.

"Okay," he answers, and once his eyes are closed, she plants one on him. Then she walks away like it was nothing, throws off her hood and sits on a large boulder.

"What the—?" Binks stumbles back.

"Well, this just got interesting," Denis says, grinning. I catch him looking at Penny again. Binks starts whistling that song about "summer lovin'."

"Oh, shut up, Binks!" Ann yells. She wipes her mouth with the sleeve of her sweatshirt and wraps her arms around her waist. A hush spreads across the schoolyard.

"Relax," Binks says, "we're not getting married or anything."

"That's for sure." Ann whips around and faces Brandi. She squints and then says, "Denis, I dare you to kiss Brandi."

Brandi looks mortified. She's still staring at her feet. She will not look up.

"Are you chicken or something?" Binks teases his friend, with a new confidence. He's rocking back and forth on his feet.

"No," Denis replies, his voice cracking. He moves closer to her. "Brandi, is it okay?"

She nods her head and closes her eyes, and in a split second he kisses her lips and it's over.

We all watch this unfold, holding in our breath.

Brandi flicks her eyes open and twists the bracelets on her arm. Her face is flushed with happiness, even under the dark sky.

Her first kiss. Come to think of it, I don't think any of us has had our first kiss, or any kiss for that matter.

"Now," she says carefully, "I dare Hari to kiss Wolf."

I'm stunned. I should have seen this coming, but I was too busy watching everything happen. I feel so panicked, so incredibly nervous. I don't think I can do this. "I don't want to play this game. It's stupid," I say.

"C'mon, seriously? Don't be such a square," Denis says.

"I'm not. It's just—"

Hari isn't looking at me whatsoever. He's staring at his feet. Does he even want to kiss me? This is so awkward.

"Going once. Going twice," Denis says, walking backwards.

My stomach is stirring like a wild electrical storm, slamming against the walls of my abdomen.

"Fine then, you're out, Wolf." Denis points.

"We should go." The words flip out of my mouth.

Hari picks up a rock and flings it across the field.

"Already?" Binks says. "But Penny hasn't kissed anyone. It's only fair."

"There's only three of you," Penny says, "and four of us."

"Then I'll kiss you." Denis steps forward.

"No! I will," Hari answers. He throws me a cool and quick glance.

"Um, I don't know if—" Penny is shuffling her feet in the dirt. Moving her head from me to Brandi and back again. She looks worried.

"Don't tell me you're a chicken too," Binks shouts.

"I'm not." Penny holds her head up high.

Everyone is now staring at Penny. Major staring. I watch Hari walk over and crack his knuckles, on both hands. I watch Penny squeeze her eyes shut. Then, Hari plants one on her mouth, not her cheek, and I don't think I'm the only one who notices that Penny is leaning in towards him, on the tips of her toes. It feels like I'm being stung by a trillion bees and hornets. Binks starts to hoot and holler and Hari is still kissing her, and then after what feels the longest kiss I've ever seen, he takes one small step back and his face is all red and he hikes back towards his friends, where we used to play Four Corners at recess. I try not to let the tears erupt. I push them back, deep down. I won't let him see me cry.

"We're done now, boys. It's been a hoot, but we have plans." Ann steps between the boys and us.

"Plans? What plans? Do you work as spies or something?" Binks says.

"We just have something to do."

"Well, see you around," Denis waves, still looking at Penny.

"See you at school," Hari says, barely looking in my direction.

I don't say anything at all.

❧

I keep moving forward but nobody is talking and we are not the same. We've changed. I'm at the back of the line and Penny is dragging her feet in front of me. Ann is walking tall like she always does and Brandi is floating in between, but we are not the same.

"We're headed to Birchwood, right?" Ann asks like nothing weird just happened.

"I guess," Brandi mutters, keeping a steady pace.

"Wolf? Penny?" Ann turns and faces us.

I pull my hood over my head. "Yeah," I say.

"I'll go," Penny mumbles.

Ann slows down so we all catch up. "Okay, good, because I think we should stick to our plan."

I know she's right but I'm trying really hard to suppress the mini-tsunami that's growing inside me. And every time I look at Penny, I think about Hari kissing her.

We eventually make our way up the trail through the Tree People lining the bottom of the mountain. We pass Birchwood, yet none of us even acknowledge it when we hike by. We keep moving onward in silence. Despite our dreadful mood, the night is surging with sounds and smells, like every living organism got the memo that summer has arrived. Unfortunately, the darn mosquitoes got the memo too.

"Am I the only one getting eaten alive over here?" Brandi snaps, slapping her bare arms. "I don't suppose you have your bug spray, Ann?"

"Negative," she says.

I find myself wishing all of the bugs would fly straight to Penny. Serves her right for kissing Hari, or letting Hari kiss her.

We keep hiking up the mountain's edge. I stop cold and suddenly when I see fresh tire tracks, new tire marks made with ATVs. I get back into mission mode. And then I spot the trees.

"Oh no!" I say into the night. "The trees! Look!" I point.

Many of the large poplars and pines have been cut. Hacked. Down to short trunks.

Ann moves to stand next to me. "They're moving so fast."

I scan the perimeter and spot orange arrows spray-painted on the ground and giant Xs on more trees up the bend. My heart drops. I'm trembling. And so are the girls. Wait, what the heck is happening? The ground quakes beneath us as we clutch on to each other for balance. The rumble continues for almost ten seconds.

"This is a really long mine blast," Penny says. She moves in closer and leans her head against Ann's back. Ann is holding on to me, tight.

I shuffle away from them, feeling annoyed. "What do you know about mine blasts anyways, Penny? Your dad never had to deal with them, counting numbers all day."

Ann shoots me a dirty look.

The ground shakes under us again, and this time it's more intense. We lock arms until it ends and bow our heads towards the pulsating ground. Once it stops, I say, "We should head back. Mom might check in on us, with the rumbles underground."

"Yeah, let's get out of here," Penny says.

"So much for the Solstice magic," I answer, staring right at Penny. Everyone got their first kiss tonight but me.

Penny drops her chin to her chest. This was not the kind of magic I was hoping for tonight. I don't know what I was expecting—just not this. Even so, I need to stop thinking about Hari and Penny. Birchwood is in serious danger and I'm so worried that my own mom is part of this. The day's events come crashing into the night. Roger. Roger + Mom. Hari + Penny.

"This really is the longest day and the shortest night," I mutter. Everything is slipping away and nothing looks the same. Not even the trees. Not with those oranges Xs marked on them and the ones that are already chopped and gone.

CHAPTER 14

We shuffle through the back sliding door and I snatch the chips and Twizzlers Mom left out for us. I give them to Brandi. "Bring these upstairs and be on the lookout. Let us know if you hear my mom."

"Okay. Good luck."

Ann and I proceed with major eavesdropping ears to her office door. It's still locked. She pulls a bobby pin from her hair and bends it into a long stick.

"A bobby pin, seriously? That's your fancy tool?"

"It works. Trust me."

Within three seconds, I hear a click and the door swings wide open.

Ann gives me her "I told you so" face.

"You continue to impress me."

She beams a smile. "Okay, so what are we looking for?" she whispers.

"A white box with a lid, and anything that can tell us if she's involved."

"Okay, so basically look through everything."

"Basically."

Mom's office is spic and span. Every surface is empty and clean and shiny. She has a small collection of plants and pictures, but nothing else is in plain view. Besides her framed realty licence certificate and a couple of thank-you cards from happy new homeowners, nothing else screams realtor or new development or proves that she's part of the Birchwood takedown.

I search around the entire perimeter and don't see the box anywhere.

I point to the file cabinet and slowly open the top drawer. I fan through the file folders quickly. They all seem to be from past jobs, things I have already heard Mom talking about. I open the bottom drawer and it's all bills, warranties, bank and insurance stuff. We then move to the small drawers on either side of her desk. Ann slides the first one open, and that's when my toe hits something under her desk. A white box.

"Ann," I whisper. "There it is." Her eyes grow big and round, and I reach down and place it on the desk.

"Hurry," she says.

I peel back the lid and I spot it right away—the folder, just like the one on the floor of Roger's Trans Am. My heart rattles.

I pick it up and read the same words printed across it: *North-wood Heights, Coming Soon* with the crown logo. My palms immediately start to sweat.

"Open it," Ann says.

Just as I'm about to do it, I hear a creak above. Footsteps. I quickly close the folder and shove it under my shirt.

"Let's bring it to my room."

"Good idea."

We put everything back in place, except for the folder. Ann locks the door from the inside, closes it shut and then follows me up the stairs. We're trying not to put any weight on the steps as we climb them. Brandi is standing by my mom's door, in total alert mode. She gives me a thumbs-up and I wave her into the bedroom. Penny's eyes are red, like she's been crying, but I cannot even think about that right now. Not when we have the proof in our hands.

"We found the file," I say after we close my bedroom door and sit on the floor.

Brandi presses her back against the bed. "Open it."

I flip it open and scan the map. My eyes bob across the page. "Oh no!" I whisper.

"Wolf? What is it?" Brandi asks.

I sigh and then I say it. "It's them. The next housing development is definitely being built over Birchwood—our favourite place on earth—thanks to my mom and Roger." I toss the folder on the floor between us.

Ann drops her head into her lap.

"Just great," Brandi says. "Tonight's been *full* of disappointments." She eyeballs Penny.

Penny gets up and reaches for a tissue.

"They're going to destroy it the way they have all of the other green spaces," I say.

Brandi hands me a Twizzler. "What do we do now?"

"I have no idea. But we have to find a way to stop this from going any further."

Penny leans in. "But Wolf, won't your mom be mad at you?"

"I don't care. I can't live without Birchwood. They will turn it into pavement and cut down every single tree," I answer.

"Even the five birch trees?" Penny asks.

Sometimes she is so clueless. "Yes, all of it! There are *some* things you can never undo," I answer with a hitch in my voice.

Ann bites into her licorice. "Okay, okay. We're all on the same page, right?"

"Brandi? What about you? What do you think?" I pick up the folder from the cream carpet.

"Um, yeah, of course," she answers, totally spaced out. Ann was right, we might have lost Brandi to the dark side. But then she says, "Unlike some people, I put my friendships first." She's back.

I try to push everything else out of my mind. It feels like a tug-of-war inside my head, but we have to protect the thriving wildlife. "Okay, let's brainstorm. They've already started chopping down some trees, so it won't be long before they bulldoze everything. We need to work fast." I grab my journal and pen from Poppy's metal lunch box that I keep tucked inside my closet.

"Interesting hiding place," Brandi says.

"Thanks, B," I reply proudly. "It was Poppy's."

Ann grabs the handle. "Did you know these lunch boxes were invented here, in Sudbury? A man named Leo May created them so miners could eat their lunch while sitting on them because they often had nowhere to sit underground."

"Of course you know this," I say.

Brandi throws a pillow at her. "You're a walking encyclopedia." She shakes her head and smiles.

"Thank you and you're welcome," Ann says.

Penny curls her lips in and tilts her head to the side. I can tell she wants to be part of the conversation. "Okay, back to business. Let's brainstorm."

Brandi's the first to make a suggestion. "What about a fasting protest?"

"Like not eating?" Ann reaches for the chips.

"Yeah. I've heard about them in social studies class. It gets attention."

"While I appreciate your suggestion, I don't think I could even go a day without eating," Ann says, waving a Dorito in the air.

We quickly axe that idea. "Any other thoughts?" I ask, ignoring Penny's side of the room.

"What about camping out there, as a protest?" Penny says, quietly.

Ann tips her head up, like she's listening intently. "You mean overnight?"

"Yeah, you know, for as long as it takes for them to change their mind."

"Well, maybe," Ann says.

"I don't think it will work," I answer. "Police could easily remove us from the premises, not to mention our parents. We need a better guarantee. Something they could not deny us."

Silence mushrooms around us. Even the chip and licorice eating has been halted.

"What about focusing on the resources? The ones they plan to destroy?" Ann says.

Brandi slinks in closer. "More details, please." She grabs another Twizzler.

Ann starts waving her hands in the air. "What if we made a list of all the wildlife and plant life that inhabit the woodland, and we could document it and see if there are any endangered or threatened species?" Both my arms erupt with truth bumps.

"I like where this is going." I start jotting it down. "I don't know about you, but I'm tired of being known as the ugly city, because of our lack of trees and vegetation. We need to preserve what we already have if we ever want a chance to lose the title."

"Exactly," Ann says. "This housing development goes completely against our regreening efforts. We can use that."

"There are so many flora that will be lost," Penny says.

"And fauna," Brandi adds.

"For sure. We could photograph it, the resources, I mean. I can borrow my dad's camera," Penny offers.

"That's good!" Ann says, with way too much enthusiasm. "We can collect our notes and photos and present it to the mayor and town councillors as evidence—like a proposal to stop the development. I've seen this kind of thing happen before at council meetings with my mom. I guess having a parent in municipal politics has its pluses!"

"I love this idea!" Brandi replies.

"Me too," I say.

"Me three," Penny says.

I put down my pen. "Okay, the truth is, even with this great plan, the chances of stopping this development are slim. I think it's critical for us to focus on what we'll lose if they destroy this woodland. We need to remind everyone about this." I flash back to the single yellow birch tree in the forest. The golden queen. At least she will be safe, for now. But what if someday someone would like to build in that area too? Someone's got to speak up for all these trees like my great-granddaddy did.

As I finally close my eyes for the night, my thoughts start with Birchwood but then quickly take me elsewhere, back to Hari and Penny. I capital-H hated watching Hari kiss Penny tonight. Brandi was kissed by her crush but I don't think that makes up for Denis volunteering to kiss Penny. Not to mention, Denis only spoke to Penny and looked at Penny all night, practically. It's obvious who Denis likes. And I'm pretty sure Ann hated kissing Binks. It looked like she wanted to heave afterwards. None of us got what we wished for tonight. Well, except for maybe Penny.

The future of Birchwood is in jeopardy, and now it seems like the pack is also in jeopardy. As I drift off to sleep, I can't help thinking that saving Birchwood might be the only way to save the pack too.

CHAPTER 15

I 'm the first one up.

"Anyone awake?" I mutter as I sit up and rustle their sleeping bags. "I was thinking, we should make that list before my mom wakes up. I wouldn't want her to overhear us."

"Wolf," Brandi moans, "why do you have to be a morning person?" She covers her head with her pillow.

Ann sits up. "Wolf is right," she says. "Let's get cracking." She throws her hair into a messy ponytail.

"Ugh." Brandi rolls over.

"I'm awake." Penny sits up with perfect hair. It's down, smooth and without a single hair out of place. Seriously?

"I thought I'd ask Grandma Houle to borrow her binoculars, to help with identifying the animals. Ann, can you do some research at the library? Find out if any of the animals we find are considered threatened or endangered? Also, I have you down for identifying every creek, pond or body of water in the area."

"I'm on it."

Brandi sits up and reaches for a Twizzler, most likely a stale Twizzler. "I can work on categorizing the trees and plants."

"Perfect."

"I can do the flowers," Penny says, nearly whispering. "And, if you like, I can take photos of all the flora and fauna. To help document it all."

"Sure, Penny. That's great. You do that," I say.

Brandi is giving me the "I'm totally with you" face.

"Okay, folks," Ann interjects. "Did you want to talk about the, you know, kissing thing?"

I consider it for a second, but Penny's face against Hari's pops into my head like lightning and I snap my journal closed. I'm totally not ready. "Let's get some breakfast," I say, and lead the way downstairs.

I hear noise in the kitchen. Pots and pans being moved around.

"My mom's up," I mumble over my shoulder as we tread quietly down the stairs.

"Act casual," Ann says.

Penny curls in her lips and makes them disappear. She looks anything but casual.

"Good morning, sleeping beauties," Mom announces while holding a spatula in the air. "How was your night? I hope you didn't get to bed *too* late." She smirks playfully.

"Nope. Not us," Brandi answers, a little too swiftly.

"Just the usual sleepover shenanigans. Nothing out of the ordinary," I add as Mom turns her back to us. "Cool it," I mouth to my friends.

All three of the girls take a deep breath. I take one too.

I feel bad lying to Mom, but I don't think I have a choice right now. And I don't feel *that* bad having seen the evidence that she's involved in the Birchwood bulldoze.

"That's pretty shocking."

"*Guinness Book of World Records* shocking, Mom."

"I'd say. I was so tired last night. I didn't hear a thing. I did however dream about being on a boat."

"That part was real," I tell her, wishing it wasn't so.

She beams the brightest smile. "The French toast should be ready soon. Have some berries while you wait. I almost forgot, I bought some whipped cream!"

Why is she trying to be mother of the year now? Because she feels guilty, I wonder? I find the whipped cream in the fridge and place it by the four small bowls of strawberries mixed with blueberries. The girls quickly dig in while I go and grab the small glasses for the orange juice. Mom scooches in beside me. "So, tell me, how do you like your new phone?"

It's hard to be mad at Mom when she's being so nice to me, but I'm really worried about Birchwood, the Tree People, the animals and the pack. That tug-of-war feeling has returned and it's moving down my chest.

"Wolf?"

"Um, it's great. Ah, and thanks again for the sleepover." I try to keep my face from showing any doubts.

"I'm really glad. You deserve it, sweetheart."

And the brutal pushing and pulling is back. Full force.

"Don't forget, we're supposed to meet Grandma this afternoon," she says before getting back to the sweet-smelling French toast.

CHAPTER 16

The crabapple trees are flowering wildly and it looks like pink confetti as we drive past them. I wish they stayed like this all summer long. I don't particularly like crabapples, not after eating way too many of them one afternoon with Brandi in her backyard, but the flowers are the prettiest. We're meeting Grandma at the creek for an afternoon picnic and fishing, to honour Poppy. I haven't said much to Mom since this morning besides one-word answers and uh-huhs. I think she's letting me get away with it because she thinks I'm tired from the sleepover, which I am. But of course that's not the whole story.

I spot Grandma up ahead as we pull over to the side of the road. She's wearing Poppy's green fishing coveralls, which are way too big for her, and a fishing hat that I'm sure she embellished herself with bird feathers and tackle. There's a picnic basket at her feet and three fishing rods leaning against her van. Mom and I step out of the car to greet her.

"My favourite mother–daughter duo! You're right on time!"

"Hi, Grandma!" I'm surprised at how loud my voice is, after being so quiet all morning.

"Granddaughter! Look at all those pins on your shoes! You have quite a collection there."

"Thanks. And look at your hat!" I point.

She smiles big and wide. "I thought I'd dazzle it up for the occasion." She twirls on her toes.

"Hello, Mother. We're here as promised."

I can tell Mom's using her even-steven tone of voice. She knows this is really important to Grandma.

"So," Grandma says, "did you hear the big news on the radio?"

"What news?" Mom asks, squinting her eyes.

Our car radio is still broken. "That was an earthquake last night. It wasn't a regular old mine blast after all!"

"An earthquake?" Mom says, noticeably surprised. "I didn't feel a thing."

"What about you, Granddaughter?"

"Nothing," I say without looking at her.

"You didn't feel it either? Well, I thought you'd be up with your friends until the sun came up!" she says, eyeballing me. "It was a trembler for sure!"

I focus on the giant bee buzzing by like it's the most

127

interesting insect in the entire universe. The last thing I want to do is talk about last night. She doesn't press me any further.

"Oh, Cathy, isn't it a beautiful Sunday? A perfect day for a picnic and some fishing," Grandma says. "I'm so glad you girls are here."

"We did promise." Mom steps ahead of us.

"Yes, well, let's get these rods in the water and see if we can get a bite. Then, we'll have a nice picnic."

"Sounds great, Grandma." I hook my arm into hers. I close my eyes and feel the sun on my cheeks.

"Wolf, you look different today," she says, leaning into me.

My eyes pop open. "What do you mean? Different how?"

"I can't describe it, exactly. It's a Grandma superpower, dear."

I stare at my feet. At the pins on my shoes. What *does* she see, I wonder? Can she tell we snuck out to meet with boys last night? Or that everything in my world feels topsy-turvy, like it's coming undone?

"I brought us some worms, and you know Poppy would want you to put your own worm on the hook, so you'll have to do that." She snickers.

"Oh, Mother, let's just get this over with," Mom mutters, over her shoulder.

"Jeepers, that's not the kind of attitude I was hoping for."

"You can't have everything."

Mom grabs a fishing rod. The tallest one. I take the shortest one.

"That's for sure," I say, wishing I could suck the words right back.

"And what is your problem this morning?" Mom twists around. "You have been in such a mood. I thought you'd be thrilled after your sleepover and new phone."

"No problem. I'm fine. Just tired, Mom."

Grandma gives me a side glance. "Last night must have been quite an all-nighter, Granddaughter."

"Let's see who catches a fish first," I reply and race off ahead.

"Now, that's the spirit!" Grandma throws a fist in the air.

We trek down to the creek, which is just a short distance from the van. A row of maple trees welcomes us, another family of Tree People, their branches stretching high above our heads. I wish I could see things from above, like them. I wonder how much more they can see. The gloomy truth is, I don't feel like I can trust many people right now, with Hari kissing Penny and my mom and Roger working together to obliterate Birchwood—nothing feels the same anymore. Everything is changing. Well, except maybe for Grandma. Thank goodness I can always count on her. But everything else feels distorted. Unbalanced. I watch the leaves rustle on the branches and I try to speak to the trees, without using words. I concentrate really hard and ask them if they can hear me.

I listen intensely, but no message comes.

Grandma catches up to me on the path and I look behind us for Mom. She's trailing far behind. She doesn't seem eager to fish. I pick a spot with a few large rocks for us to sit on and dig into the Styrofoam bowl full of worms. I pull out a short, fat one, then quickly spear it with my hook and cast my line into the water. It zings a few feet away and plops into the calm green creek. I tilt my head back and the maple leaves are glistening in the lilac sky, tinged with a sunburst of orange sun, and somehow, for a split second, surprisingly everything feels just right again, on the inside and the outside. I hope Poppy can see me right now.

Only Grandma catches a fish. Actually, she catches three little brook trout and she's so happy she's whistling while she wraps the last one in newspaper, which she tucks into her small blue cooler to keep cold. We wash our hands in the creek and then sit on the ground to have our picnic lunch. Mom tries to convince Grandma to sit at the nearby picnic table, but she says Poppy would never have sat there, so we'll do it the way he did, on the rocks, at the edge of the water.

Grandma packed everything in threes: three tuna sandwiches wrapped in wax paper, three tiny Tupperware containers with coleslaw, three large pickles and three slices of apple pie, with iced tea in a large, green thermos and three matching red cups. It really is a perfect summer's day. You'd never think the world around me was falling apart. Even my mom seems to be enjoying herself, despite her earlier protest. She's rolled up the sleeves of her white cotton blouse and she's soaking up the sun too—dangling her feet in the water.

"Well, this is swell. I know how busy you are these days, so this afternoon is extra special for me. Positively." Grandma pops in the last bite of her sandwich.

"It's nice, Grandma. I think Poppy would be very happy to see us all here."

"Yes, he would, Wolf. I think he'd be especially pleased to see your mom fishing."

Mom drops her chin towards her chest. I remember that Mom was really sad when Poppy died. She didn't speak to anyone for almost a week and she stayed in bed with the door closed. Grandma once told me that she was his favourite because they always went fishing together when she was little, but not to repeat that because Auntie Beth and Uncle Kevin would be sad about it, even though they already knew it to be true. I don't remember Mom ever fishing or liking the outdoors. She's never taken me camping or even on a picnic at the beach. It's like she's allergic to nature or something. During one of our many sleepovers, Grandma told me that when Mom was my age, she was always outside and barefoot, running wild into the woods. Supposedly, her favourite animal was the black bear and she used to hide in the woods and look for them so she could write things about them in a small, black spiral note-book, like a bear-loving Jane Goodall. She says Mom was never afraid of them, even when they went blueberry picking deep inside the forest, near the Levack mine. I wonder what made her change so much.

"Mother, please. I'm here. I fished. I'm eating your sandwich."

"I just mean it's nice to see you in this environment again. In nature. You used to love—"

"Not this again."

"I totally agree. Mom rarely spends time in the woods. I think everyone should," I say, pleased with myself.

"Right-o, Granddaughter." Grandma points at me with her pickle. "It keeps us young. Nature is the only medicine I need."

"Cheers to that!" I swing my cup to meet hers and then to Mom's. But Mom doesn't cheers us back.

"Oh, Cathy, you should spend your time growing trees, not chopping them down. That job sure has changed you."

Mom sighs loudly. "You have no idea what's changed me."

"I'm trying to understand. You never let me in."

"And why should I, after all this time?" Mom's tone is not even-steven anymore. Not one bit.

"Well, on second thought, it might be the pickle up your butt," Grandma says, biting into her pickle. "Or maybe it's that new boyfriend of yours."

Suddenly, there are twenty angry lines dancing around Mom's mouth. She purses her lips into a sharp point.

"Finish up, Wolf. We're leaving."

"But I haven't had my pie," I moan, raising my clean fork.

"Take it with you, Granddaughter." Grandma knows she went too far this time.

I'm sitting in the car with my eyes glued to Grandma. My head and shoulders are swivelled around to look behind as we drive away, while the seatbelt digs into my chest. She's no longer wearing her hat and she doesn't wave goodbye at us like she usually does. She's staring out onto the water that's touching the sky. I wish she'd look back. I want to wave goodbye.

Mom's driving fast. As upset as I am with her about Birchwood, I also know when to stand down. I decide to hold my tongue as we continue along the lengthy stretch of road.

I watch Grandma become a speck of green and disappear into the bright summer sun.

CHAPTER 17

Our last week of school should be interesting after what happened on the night of the Summer Solstice.

Brandi is the first of the pack to arrive at our spot on Monday. She looks as eager as I am to be here.

"Hey."

"Hey," I say back. "You okay?"

"Great. You?" she asks.

"No comment."

"Seriously, Wolf? I can't believe Penny." She leans against the brick wall.

I whip my backpack off my shoulders, let it fall to the ground. "I know. She could have said no."

"Exactly."

"I think he likes her too," I say.

Brandi crinkles her nose. "Hari? I really don't think so."
She shakes her head from side to side. "I think Hari likes you."

"He kissed her," I answer.

"I know, but boys do stupid things," she pings back. "I think
Denis likes her and I think she likes Denis. That's what I think."

"I don't know about that," I say, even though deep down, I
kind of have the same feeling too.

"I know it." She twists her large hoop earring. "This must
be what Esmeralda meant, you know. About a friend breaking
another friend's heart. Remember?"

I offer her a sympathetic smile. I don't want Esmeralda to
be right about anything. We continue to sit in silence while
sounds of the schoolyard grow louder around us.

Ann rushes up, her arms swinging wildly. She trips over her
feet but quickly recovers without a tumble to the ground. "Did
you hear?" she says.

"Hear what?" we ask at the same time.

"There was an accident . . . two miners . . . they're trapped!"
She's trying to catch her breath.

"Oh no." A spike of worry pricks my heart. "But wait,
remember the blasts on Saturday night? Grandma said it was
actually an earthquake. Do you think it happened then?"

Ann creases her forehead. "I'm not sure. My dad was called
out for search and rescue in the middle of the night last night."

"Do you know who they are?" Brandi asks, both hands flat
against her chest.

"They haven't released any names yet. But it's not looking good. At least that's what I heard Mom say on the phone this morning."

"Oh! I hate it when this happens. It's always the worst news ever." My voice cracks. "B! Was your dad working last night?" I ask, panicked.

"No." Brandi starts pacing. "He wasn't. But everyone knows everyone. No matter what, it won't be good," she says.

The bell rings and it startles me. It startles us all. Nobody makes a move. We're all still processing the news.

Then Ann heaves her knapsack over her shoulder. "I'll see you in third period," she says.

"Lunch," Brandi replies. "We'll talk about it then." Then she asks, "Hey wait. Where's Penny?"

"No idea," I answer and hurry to homeroom.

When I step into class, I glance at Hari's desk, but he's not here either. I wonder if Hari and Penny are together, skipping school, and then I tell myself to knock it off. There are more serious things going on. Two miners are trapped in the dark, possibly under rocks and muck. I need to stop being so selfish.

It's not until after lunch that Mrs. Flattery gets a knock on the door from Principal Hatfield and steps into the hall to speak with her. Then Jenna Mora (the biggest blabbermouth in the whole class) says she overheard them speaking on her way back from the washroom. By the time Jenna makes it back to her seat, Mr. Patel's name is on everyone's lips. Hari's dad. Mrs. Flattery walks back into the classroom and wipes her tears. She tries to be discreet. She doesn't tell us what she learned, but we already know.

I just keep staring at Hari's desk.

My eyes lock onto Denis Gervais's from across the room. His eyes start to water and he plunks his head down on his desk. I lower mine too and close my eyes, feeling like the waves have sucked me down into the bottom of the darkest sea.

CHAPTER 18

After the news spreads across the whole school, nobody speaks to anybody. It's like we can't even look at each other or we'll just start to cry, and so we keep our heads down. Our teachers let us read whatever we want in our afternoon classes. We're even allowed to take new books out from the library, even though it isn't our regular weekly scheduled time. I choose a classic, *Emily of New Moon*, because I need comfort. The last time this happened was a couple of years ago. Wendy was in a class below me and she moved away to another city after her dad's accident. She never came back to school after he died. I wonder if Hari will leave too. Sadness floods me like a horrible flu.

School ends before I have a chance to talk to the girls because Ann had to help with the kindergarteners at lunch. It was her turn. All the grade eights have to help in their senior year. And Brandi was asked to answer the phones during lunch for Secretary Francie, who's retiring soon. Brandi does have the most friendly phone voice, but I'm sure that wasn't the case today. Penny never showed up.

The person I want to talk to the most is Grandma Houle, so I leave for her house as soon as the bell rings. The sun is blazing hot and the sky is perfectly blue. It should be raining. It should be storming. How could it be such a beautiful day without a single cloud, when the whole town is heartbroken?

Grandma opens the door slowly and I fall into her arms.

"My dear girl. I heard the terrible news."

"Oh, Grandma, Mr. Patel—" The tears start gushing.

"I know, sweetheart. Come in. Come in." She holds me and rocks me, until all of my tears are on the outside. She wipes my face with her soft, wrinkled hands. "Wolf, I know how sad you are for Hari. I am too. It's a terrible thing to happen. Absolutely, positively terrible."

"But how can these things *still* happen? I thought they did tests and studies to make sure it was safer underground."

"I know, dear. They've made improvements, but we still have a long way to go."

"Mining is so dangerous," I say. "Even if you don't die down there, you die from it eventually, like Poppy." More tears drench my face.

"Oh, Wolf. I know. We might be spread out across this town, but we're one big family. It hurts us all when a miner dies. It's a really, really sad day." Grandma hugs me hard and I cry some more. Mostly, I cry for Hari, because I know he's going to miss his dad and nothing can fill a hole that big. I think of my grandpa, who I still miss, every single day.

Grandpa, like Mr. Patel, was an immigrant to this country. Grandma says they both came here in search of a better life. Poppy came all the way from Scotland to find work, which I find really hard to believe. Why would you leave Scotland and cross the sea for a city with only one bowling alley and a drive-in theatre? Grandma says men from all over the world came here to mine our nickel, that our resource town drew in immigrants from all over the world looking for a better life. She said you could make a really good living, but it wasn't without its risks.

Grandpa was sick for a long time before he passed away. Near the end, his breathing was so laboured, he sounded like Darth Vader. He used to say that he was the actor who played him. "The secret's out, Loo Loo." That's what he called me. He always tried to make me laugh, no matter what, even when he was struggling to breathe and his body was full of arthritis. Grandpa was only seventeen years old when he started working underground. That's a lot of dark days extracting ore. He and Grandma were married for fifty-one years.

"Here's some more Kleenex, darling."

"Thanks, Grandma. Thanks for always being here."

"It's my favourite thing in the whole wide world."

I hug her one more time. I'm pretty sure I don't have any tears left, so I blow my nose and sit up against the sofa.

"All you can do is be a good friend to Hari. That's what he needs now."

"You're right." I say.

"Now, now. Let's fill our bellies with sweet bannock and cedar tea. That combination makes everything better." She kisses my stained cheek.

CHAPTER 19

After eating Grandma's delicious bannock plus raspberry rhubarb pie, my heart still feels broken. It probably will be for a long time, but the sugar makes my head less foggy.

I tell Grandma I want to walk home even though she really wants to drive me. I tell her I need the fresh air. I know Mom is working late tonight because she left me a note telling me so on the kitchen counter this morning. Before I leave Grandma's house with my backpack full of containers filled with soup and stew and homemade muffins, I remember to ask her if I can borrow her binoculars, and she doesn't think twice before saying yes.

Once I get home, I decide the best thing to do to stop my heart from hurting is to keep my mind moving, so I get to work. I start to write down all of the animals I remember seeing around Birchwood.

This is my list so far:

Brown rabbits
Eagles
Crows
Ravens
Foxes
Black bears
Painted turtles
Blue jays
Robins
Squirrels and chipmunks
Owls (we heard them but haven't seen them yet)

After I'm done with the list, I reheat some chicken soup, put my muffin on a plate and climb the stairs to my room. I consider calling Hari on my new phone, and then I think, no way, what if I say the wrong thing and what if he wants me to leave him alone not just because of his dad, but because of the Penny kiss? So I decide to write him a letter instead to let him know how sorry I am for him and his family. And, like Grandma said, this is one way I can show him that I'm a good friend. I start over three times until I like the way his name is written and then I just keep going:

Dear Hari,

I heard about your dad this afternoon at school, and I'm SO sorry. Your dad was always nice to me, whenever I saw him. He always called me "Little Lagacé" and tipped his ball cap when he said it, and he'd always bring my grandma a batch of garlic from his garden every fall. He also helped to push my mom out of the snow once when she got stuck on the road. Please know that ~~I~~ we are all thinking about you: me, Brandi, Ann and Penny, my mom and Grandma Houle too. Everyone at school actually. We're all so sorry Hari.

~~Your friend always,~~

Always,

Wolf

Writing this letter makes me feel a tiny bit better. I'm not sure how I'm going to give it to him yet. The last thing he said to me on Saturday was "See you at school, Wolf." I wish we could go back to that night, to Summer Solstice, and alter what's happened. Everything changed on that day: the pack, finding out about Mom and Roger's plan for Birchwood, and now Mr. Patel . . . If only we could go back in time.

CHAPTER 20

Mom must have gotten home very late because I didn't hear her come in and I'm usually a light sleeper. I think she feels guilty because she's making me pancakes before school this morning and that's super rare on a weekday. I can smell the sweet scent of batter sizzling in the pan. Wait a minute. I try to remember what day of the week it is, and I pop my eyes open and spring out of bed. These are not guilty pancakes after all! I rush to my desk calendar and find it circled: Tuesday, June 24. Today is my birthday. Today is my *thirteenth* birthday! I'm a teenager. I'm a *real* teenager.

I stare at myself in the mirror to see if I look like a teen. My eyes are puffy from yesterday's many tears and my hair is sticking up but I still really like it. It feels weird to be celebrating after yesterday, but I can't help but feel a slow rising thrill. I'm thirteen. THIRTEEN! I make my way downstairs.

"There you are! I thought I was going to have to spritz you with water to wake you up this morning."

"I'm up, I'm up."

She looks up from the pan. "A true teenager, that's for sure."

"I guess so," I say, my pride slipping into the faintest smile.

"Happy Birthday pancakes!" She plops them down in front of me. They smell so good. And then I spy a brand new bottle of *real* maple syrup sitting on the table.

"Oh! Thanks, Mom."

She pops open the new bottle and hands it to me.

"So, are you excited to finally be a teen?" She leans in closer and our knees touch under the table.

I breathe out my nose and move my legs away from hers. I am. At least I think I am, but I wish Mom would give me a little space right now. It's kind of embarrassing.

"In a way." I feel like I've been waiting my whole life for this day. "But it's hard not to be sad for Hari," I say, with my elbows on the table, my cheeks now sitting in my hands.

"I know, honey. It's awful. Grandma called me last night at work and told me how upset you were. I'm sorry I was so late. I wish I could have been here." She pours orange juice into a small glass. "We had a meeting with some business people who travelled from Toronto—"

"I'd rather not hear about work today, okay?" I interrupt her.

"All right, birthday girl. I can honour that! Finish up your breakfast and then take a peek outside. Grandma dropped something off for you early this morning, while the moon was still out."

"What is it?" I ask, with a mouth full of buttery goodness covered in real maple syrup. I set down my fork and poke my head out the door because I'm just too curious to wait.

"Oh my golly gosh!" I say through my mouthful. I can't believe it. It's a baby blue Supercycle twelve speed! "It's SO beautiful!"

"It really is!" Mom's face lights up. "She's been hiding it in her shed for three weeks hoping you wouldn't see it until today."

"I had no idea!"

"I bought this to go along with it." Mom hands me a lock. "Let's not have a repeat performance from last year. Promise me you will put it away in the shed, every day."

"I will, Mom. I promise! I'll never forget again." And to my surprise, I press myself into her chest and give her a real, squishy hug. I rush back to the table and take another huge bite of pancake and barrel through the door to jump on my brand new bike. I leave the rest of my fluffy pancakes behind.

The wind is blowing against my face and I'm pumping so fast to make it up the large hill. I finally reach the top and let myself roll down, my legs off of the pedals, my hands still on the bars. I wish I could ride my bike all day. It makes such a soft clicking sound as I zip down the hill. I absolutely love it! It's beyond perfect.

I make a pit stop over at Grandma's house before I go to school. I want to thank her for my birthday gift. But when I get there, her van is gone, which is unusual because every morning she listens to her radio show, *Morning North*, while drinking her coffee on the porch. It's what she does. She only plans appointments in the afternoon. I happen to notice that her garden is getting full of weeds too. I need to remember to offer my help. I leave her a note and stick it inside her mailbox.

> *Dear Grandma,*
> *Thank you for the most beautiful bike I've ever seen!*
> *Love, Wolf xo*

The pack is waiting for me by the main entrance with gigantic smiles.

"There's the birthday girl," Brandi says.

Penny gives me a thumbs-up. "Nice wheels!"

I'm surprised, but I don't feel angry towards her like before. I can't tell if it's birthday magic or because of what happened with Hari's dad, but it's replaced the heavy boulder in my heart with a pebble.

Ann's got one hand on her hip, acting fake-mad. "What took you so long this morning? Joyriding or something?"

"Your bike is beautiful, Wolf," Brandi says.

"Thanks! It's from Grandma Houle." I snap the lock in place.

Brandi sits on my bike and pinches the brakes. "I seriously need a Grandma Houle."

"Okay, the bell's going to ring any second and we want to give you this." Ann hands me a beautifully wrapped package.

"Wow! You didn't need to do this. It's been so bonkers."

Penny steps closer. "We wanted to bring it to your sleep-over but it wasn't finished yet . . ." Her voice trails off into a whisper.

I pull back the purple tissue paper. Inside, I find a journal with a painted jet-black mountain and a forest on it. Sitting at the base of the mountain are a fox, a deer, a rabbit and a wolf. The colours are so bright: turquoise, chartreuse and pur-ple with a pink full moon and our cabin there, surrounded by the five birch trees. It also has this printed along the bottom: FOREVER BIRCHWOOD.

All three of them say it at the same time: "Forever Birchwood."

"Ah! I love it!"

"It's us, Wolf, all of us!" Brandi cries, clapping her hands together.

"Seriously?"

"Yeah, I'm the fox," Ann says, "and Penny's the deer."

"That leaves the rabbit." Brandi points to her chest. "I know I'm always bouncing around." She bobs her head, playfully. "Do you like it? We know how much you like writing and"— Brandi looks excitedly at the other girls—"Penny painted it, but it was Ann's idea, and I sewed the pages into it with special string and then Ann wrapped it. It was a total group effort."

I hug the journal against my heart. This feels like we're on our way back to normal again. Like we might be able to really work together to save Birchwood after all, and keep the pack intact.

"Happy birthday, Wolf," Penny says, with a warm smile.

I half smile back.

The bell rings and we make plans to meet at lunch. I'm on cloud nine as I'm walking to my locker with the journal in my hands after riding my new bike to school; even thinking of Mom's pancakes with real maple syrup fills me with happiness. I let this feeling carry me forward until it stops cold. I spot Hari's locker beside mine, and all of my joy quickly drains and it's replaced with sorrow. I wonder how he's doing. I wonder how his mom is doing. I wonder if I'll ever see him again or if he'll disappear, like Wendy. I slide the journal on the top shelf of my locker, click it shut and hurry into homeroom.

I almost immediately back out again when I see Hari sitting in his chair, looking down at his desk. I can't believe he's at school. He's reading something. It looks like a card. My legs bring me to him, like I don't even have control over my body anymore. He's sitting there and my heart hurts so much for him. And—

"Wolf, hi," he says, and glances away.

"Hari. I'm . . . I'm so sorry, for your dad. I mean, I'm sorry about your dad—"

"Thanks," he says, turning up his face for a quick moment, yet long enough for me to see that the rims of his eyes are red.

"I'm surprised to see you here, at school. But, I'm glad to see you, I mean."

"My mom thought it'd be good for me, to be around friends."

"That makes sense." I clutch the edge of his desk.

"With school over in three days, and grade eight and everything. To be honest, it's hard to be home right now."

"For sure." I try to think of something nice to say. Something that doesn't sound completely stupid. "I wrote you a letter."

"You did?" He looks up.

I'm now looking straight into his eyes. "Yes."

"Where is it? The letter."

"It's at home." Tucked inside my secret hiding spot in Poppy's old lunch box. "I'll give it to you after school." My cheeks are burning, even with his sad eyes peering into mine.

"Okay," he answers, with the slightest, quietest smile.

"After school," I tell him again, before Mr. Butterworth orders us to get seated. I rush to my desk with my stomach making mini-cartwheels and somersaults. I glance back and Hari's still looking at me. So I point to my shirt and to Mr. Butterworth, and mouth the words, "He's wearing it again?" I roll my eyes and make the silliest face.

Hari cracks a smile and I really hope I'm being a good friend, the kind he needs right now.

I don't tell the girls about him at lunch, besides the fact that he's back because his mom wanted him to finish the year with his friends. They don't push for more information. I'm not upset with Penny anymore. Mr. Patel's accident put things in perspective. Some things are more important than others. Like being a good friend to Hari, whether he likes Penny or not. Maybe being thirteen helps you realize things like that.

CHAPTER 21

I lock up my bike and go straight to my room. In my closet, I reach up for Poppy's lunch box. I pull out the letter I wrote for Hari. I reread it and fold it back up and make a tiny envelope to slide it in, using the comics from last week's *Northern Star*. I slide the letter into the handmade envelope and decide to make him something else. I can't make him a friendship pin because that's a pack thing, so I decide to make him a bracelet using some leftover leather string I have and a single yellow cylinder bead. I wonder what the pack would say if they saw me now? I assume that Ann would not be impressed. Brandi would definitely give me two thumbs-up. I'm not really sure what Penny would say.

I pick yellow because it's the colour that most represents happiness and I want more than anything for Hari to feel happy again. I've never made anything for a boy before. I slide the bracelet inside the envelope, take a deep breath and pick up my phone to call him.

"Hello?" he says.

"It's Wolf." I'm relieved and panicky at the same time.

"Hey."

"So, about that letter. I can meet you somewhere and give it to you."

"Turns out I have to go to my cousin's for supper and then we're going to the funeral home, for a planning meeting," he says, his voice scratchy.

"I'm sorry, if—"

"Can we meet later, like eight o'clock at the school?"

"Yes," I answer without hesitating. "I'll meet you there."

I hang up the phone realizing my breath is short and shallow and my head is woozy. I breathe in deeply to help bring the oxygen back to my brain and tuck Hari's letter back into my secret hiding place for now. I click the latch shut and stuff it under my bed, for easy access. My door swings open.

"Mom! Some privacy, please?"

"Sorry, Wolf. I want us to get going. I made reservations for dinner and you need to get changed."

"Changed? Reservations? Where are we going?"

"The Cedar Ridge Restaurant. I told you this morning. Roger's meeting us there, remember? Hurry up, please."

I vaguely remember her mentioning something, calling after me while I hopped on my new bike and drove off. But this isn't what I want to do on my birthday. "Mom, please! Do we have to?"

"Listen, I know it's been a hard week, with Mr. Patel's passing, but I want us to spend time together, all three of us. We won't be out late, I promise." She leans in and gives me a side hug.

"Well, okay," I say, begrudgingly. "As long as it's not a long dinner."

"Scout's honour." She flashes me a genuine smile.

It's kind of hard to figure out how to balance the fact that Mom is being such a great mom these days against her and Roger's master plan to extinguish Birchwood. After tonight, after I give Hari this letter, I have to get the pack back on track. And I need to explain to Mom why Birchwood is so important to me. She needs to know.

We're sitting in a booth at the back of the Cedar Ridge Restaurant, and you'd never know that it's sunny outside because the room is so dark and there are a trillion glasses hanging from the ceiling above a large bar and several ugly paintings of sailboats on the walls. We've never been to this restaurant before. On special occasions, we always go to Pat & Mario's because Mom says they have the best Caesar salad. She also lives for their garlic bread.

Roger has his arm around Mom the whole time. I haven't been able to enjoy my chicken fingers and fries because nobody wants to see their mom involved in any PDA.

"Ahem, Wolf." Roger wipes his mouth with his napkin and stuffs it under his plate. He clears his throat again. "So, I know I should probably wait until after dinner"—he laughs, nervously—"but I just can't, so, here it is." He pulls out a small blue box from his pocket. He looks nervous again, fidgeting with his watch.

"Roger?" Mom leans forward with her elbows on the table.

He plunks down the box in front of me and I ogle it. I admit that I want to see what's inside, but I don't want to like it, whatever it is. Not really.

"What are you waiting for, Wolf? Open it!" Mom pushes it towards me. I reach for it and slowly pop it open. Inside, I find a delicate gold chain with a golden pendant attached to it.

"It's a tree." He sucks in his top lip and squirms in his seat. "I know how much you love them, and, I thought, well I thought—I hope you like it." He stops talking.

"It's beautiful!" Mom sings. She takes the box from my hands and dangles the pendant in my face.

"It's a willow tree." Roger points. "I used to climb one in my granny's backyard. She had a tire swing and everything."

I'm tongue-tied. I feel like my words are suspended on a distant faraway cloud.

Mom glances at me. "Wolf. What do you say?"

I comb my short bangs with my fingers. I still can't find my words.

"Dang it, I forgot to give you the card first." He hands me a pink envelope and I slide the card out very slowly. On the cover it reads *Happy 13th Birthday!* I open it and I'm surprised to find a written message besides the typical signature under the typed birthday greeting. His handwriting is neat. Neater than mine, even.

> *Dear Wolf, I hope we can become pals, starting today.*
> *Birthdays are a perfect day for starting new things. R*

I shut the card and tuck it back into the envelope. "Thanks," I chirp. A teeny smile slinks across my face. It fades away quickly. I'm not sure I totally believe his willow tree story but I kind of want to, at least for Mom's sake. And the necklace is really pretty. Even I can see that. The card and the necklace are actually thoughtful. Very thoughtful. Birthdays *are* full of surprises.

"You're such a good guy." Mom kisses his cheek. Once. Then twice. Gross and gross.

I snap the jewellery box closed and hold it in my hands, turning it over while I study them both from across the table. Mom really likes him. And I think he really likes her too. Roger's proven that he's not terrible at buying gifts and writing thoughtful messages in cards with perfect penmanship. If it weren't for the fact that they are behind the plan to destroy Birchwood, maybe I could even learn to like him.

CHAPTER 22

I'm back from the restaurant and I'm officially beat. Birthdays are full of emotions. Especially thirteen-year-old birthdays. But I still have one more thing to do. I tell Mom I'm just going out for a quick bike ride. I arrive at the school and perch myself in the corner, where most of the other grade eights hang out during the day. Well, the ones who play Dungeons & Dragons anyway, which I never got into, but whatever floats your boat, as Grandma would say. I watch the swirl of chip bags and wrappers torpedoing around me. Why don't people put their garbage in the bins? I leap up to snatch the multicoloured wrappers and stuff them deep inside the basket of my bicycle. Around me, the seagulls dip their heads across the pavement, diving for crumbs and discarded lunches. It's been a while now and I start to worry Hari's not coming. My purple Swatch points to 8:21 p.m. Maybe he changed his mind or maybe his mom said she wanted him to stay home. I should probably go back and concentrate on trying to stop my whole world from collapsing.

Besides, he totally likes Penny. He *kissed* Penny. What am I even doing here? My stomach is doing backflips. Unsteady quadruple-axel backflips. And why do I feel like I could possibly upchuck? It's the cake. It had way too much frosting. Pink frosting. I don't even like Hari. Do I? Do I like him?

I decide to go home. I shove the envelope back into my pocket, flick my kickstand, and right before I push off, I see him. He flings me a quick wave and my hands instantly feel clammy. Hari starts jogging my way and I completely abandon my plan to go home.

"I'm sorry I'm late," he says, catching his breath. "Things took longer than I thought."

"That's okay. Are you okay? I mean, how was it, at the funeral home?" Inside, I cringe. What a stupid question.

"Well, uh, kinda awkward. Mom cried the whole time and my brother has barely talked since everything happened and, uh honestly, it's nice to be out of the house right now."

"I'm sure. I'm so sorry."

"I know." He brushes his hair off his face. "So, where's this letter?" he asks, with a glimmer in his eyes.

I suddenly feel my knees wobble. I pull the envelope out of my pocket.

"It's nothing, really. You know. I just wanted you to know that I was thinking of you and everything. I didn't know you were going to be at school so I wrote it because I wanted you to know."

"Just hand it over already," he says, in his Hari way.

And then he opens it and reads it, right there in front of me. I watch his eyes skim the page from side to side and my heart speeds like a maniac, and then I see his face break out in a humongous smile and then he says, "So, your pack was thinking about me, your mom *and* your grandma?"

"Yup, all of us." I feel my face redden. I wonder if he means Penny too?

"Thanks, Wolf." He folds it carefully. "It's really nice what you said about my dad." He pauses. "It's nice to hear how much people liked him." His voice is shaky.

"We all did, Hari. And I want you to know that we're all here for you." I'm totally relieved that part is over with. I really wasn't sure what he would think of my letter. Too sentimental? Not sentimental enough, given the serious circumstances?

"And, what's inside here?" He squeezes the bottom of the envelope.

Out comes the bracelet I made, with the brown leather string and single yellow bead.

"So, yeah, I made you something," I say as my whole chest pounds.

"Cool. I've never worn a bracelet before."

I exhale. "Let me help you get it on."

And then I make a knot, the kind that Poppy showed me, the kind of knot that lets you slide the bracelet on and off, if you want to.

"Thanks. I like it," he says, and I think he means it and he's not just being polite.

My face flushes. "I'm glad."

He looks at me and I can feel it burrow all the way into my belly. He smiles the kind of smile that sends rainbows to my heart, and then slowly he fumbles his fingers into mine and my hand is now in his hand.

"Thanks for letting me kinda forget the hard stuff right now."

I feel his eyes on me. I glance away quickly, tempted to count the seagulls, but I resist.

"I wish I could change what happened," I say.

"I know. Me too. More than anything. I wish I could go back to that morning, actually. Even for five minutes."

"Five minutes. That doesn't seem like too much to ask for."

"Yeah. A lot can happen in five minutes."

"Tell me, what would happen in your five minutes?"

"Well, this might sound kinda corny." He rubs his shoe in the dirt. "But I would hug my dad, you know, hug him goodbye like I used to do before he left for work. He actually tried to hug me that morning, but I wouldn't let him, and now I regret it so much. More than anything." He lowers his gaze.

"Hari. I'm so sorry. I wish you could get those five minutes back too."

"Thanks," he says, wiping his eyes quickly with his sleeve.

We sit on the concrete step and don't say another word for a really long time. I watch the tiny stars ink the giant sky, while Hari holds my hand in his. We listen to crickets sing and the baseball game in progress, not far away. I can smell the lilacs in full bloom. It's still warm, but not hot. The mosquitoes aren't even out yet and I could seriously stay here forever, with my stomach twisting and my skin tingling and . . .

"I should get going," he says. "I don't want to, but my mom will get worried if—"

"I understand."

He squeezes my hand before he lets it go.

He walks me back to my street, while I push my bike at turtle speed. We walk back in the most non-awkward silence. The comfortable kind, even.

"Wolf," he stops. "Happy birthday! I just remembered. It was on the announcements today. I'm such a jerk."

"You have a lot on your mind. I nearly forgot it was my birthday today too. I had to check the calendar," I say, both my hands crossed over my heart.

"You did?" He laughs and tilts his head to the side. I'm not sure he believes it.

"Yup."

"Thirteen, right? You finally caught up to me again."

"Thirteen," I nod. I've wanted to be thirteen my whole life.

"So, what do you think of it so far?" he asks.

"Day One is pretty special." I say shyly, looking past his ear.

The silence rolls back between us. Hari shuffles his feet against the pavement.

"Wolf, I uh, I want you to know, I didn't want to kiss Penny that night, well not exactly."

"Why did you, then? You weren't exactly dared. You volunteered." I try to keep my voice really even.

"I know." He sighs. "That's why I feel so bad about it. The truth is, I uh, kind of wanted to kiss someone else."

"You did?" I stop pushing my bike.

He turns towards me and pauses. "Yeah."

"So, someone else then?" I pinch the handlebars and hold my breath.

"Yeah. And it might or might not be her birthday today." His dark amber eyes are glowing.

"Really?"

"Totally."

"Well, thanks for letting me know, then." I feel my cheeks starting to colour again.

He exhales. "I've been meaning to clear that up."

I'm totally swimming in his eyes—in the deep end. Night swimming in the lake, with only the stars above us.

"Thanks for this." He shows me the bracelet. "And the letter, too."

"You're welcome." I feel my whole face flush one last time. He smiles a huge ginormous smile and I smile a huge ginormous smile back and I turn on my heels and up my driveway and I'm one hundred percent sure that he's more than just my friend.

I hear him sprint down the road and then I look up at the wide-open canopy of stars. I find the little dipper and the big one too. The North Star is there, like always, shining super bright. I want to remember exactly what the sky looks like tonight. I want to save it for eternity. Despite all of the heartache from before, my thirteenth birthday turned out to be the most special birthday of my entire life.

A white moth tickles my cheek and I manage to remember to park my bike in the shed and lock it up. But not before making a wish on a shooting star.

Birthday magic, I whisper to myself.

CHAPTER 23

The rest of the week passes quickly enough, and then just like that, it's the last day of school! It's circled on my calendar with lots of exclamation marks. Not only is it the last day, but it's the last day of junior school! It seems so hard to believe! As much as Rockwood Public felt small at times, I'm really going to miss it. I've been a student there my whole school life. When I think back, it went super slow and super fast, all at the same time. It seems weird to think about starting somewhere new in the fall. It's such a big decision.

I'm guessing there might be some tears today. At least we'll be able to zero in on saving Birchwood after classes end. That's what I'm going to think about if I feel sad at all. We have a serious mission to complete.

As I'm getting ready, the phone rings and I stumble across my room to answer it. I nearly trip on a large pile of clothes.

"Hello."

"Wolf, it's Penny. Penny Whitmore."

"I know which Penny you are, Penny," I say.

"Right. Sorry."

I can tell she still feels uncomfortable. She's talking super fast. Hearing her voice actually makes me feel bad too. I'm realizing that I haven't been a good friend to her since that night at the school. It's not like it was *her* idea to kiss Hari. I think I can forget the Penny/Hari kiss now—especially after talking to Hari the other night. Now that I know how he *really* feels.

"Wolf, I've been wanting to talk to you alone but we haven't had the chance," she says. "I'm really sorry. I didn't mean to hurt you. I don't even like Hari. Not like that, anyway." I can hear her sniffling on the other end of the line.

"It's okay, Penny. I know you didn't mean to hurt anyone."

"You do? So, you forgive me then?"

"Yeah, I do. And I'm sorry for the way I've been acting too. Even if Hari did like you, that wouldn't be your fault. Let's move on, okay?"

"That reminds me of my second reason for calling. My dad took the camera to Halifax, so I won't be able to bring it with me after school to document the wildlife in pictures. Sorry."

"It's okay. We'll just have to draw what we see for now."

"Thanks for understanding. I've really missed you."

"Me too," I say. "I'll see you soon."

Right after school, I plan to go to the woods to continue our research and see if Roger's crew has advanced in the demolition of the forest. I'm so scared to find out. It's been almost a week since my sleepover, and with Hari's dad and my birthday, we haven't been back yet.

The girls are already waiting for me. I lock up my bike and book it to the field.

"Late again, Lagacé?" Brandi peeps.

"The bell hasn't rung yet."

"Ladies," Denis Gervais hollers as he strolls by with Binks.

Brandi freezes. Penny stares at her hands and I notice her crimson cheeks.

"Where's your third musketeer?" Ann asks.

"Hari? He's not coming again today." His voice dips. "Some of his family is heading home since the funeral is over."

I try not to show my disappointment, while all eyes land on me. A Frisbee zings past us, and then a second one. It's a frenzy in the schoolyard, that's for sure. Kids are running around with their yearbooks in hand, trying to get everyone in the graduating class to sign it.

"Let's focus," I say, barely able to ignore the last-day hoopla for five seconds. "After today, it's full-on mission mode, right?"

"Of course," Brandi says.

Penny points. "What she said."

Brandi gives her an obvious eye roll. I guess Penny didn't call Brandi this morning before school. Or maybe she did and Brandi's not ready to forgive her.

"I brought my *Science Is Everything* magazines." Ann pulls them out of her bag. "This will show you exactly how to categorize the resources, with proper headings and whatnot." She hands us each one. "I won't be able to be there until after my sister's party. It's her high school grad celebration tonight, with the grandparents, aunts and uncles. I've been warned it's a must-attend for every McFadden." She sighs.

"Have fun with that," Brandi says, "but don't worry, we've got you covered."

"What time are we meeting?" Penny asks.

I dodge another Frisbee. "Let's go right after school. Maybe Roger's crew will finish early on a Friday afternoon."

"Wolf, I've been wondering, have you tried to talk to your mom yet?" Penny asks. "Maybe if she knew how much Birchwood meant to you, to us—"

"Well, not exactly. I've been trying to figure out how to bring it up. To tell her how I feel. But I know she thinks it's helping to change our ugly city reputation. That's what they both think. Her *and* Roger."

Penny shuffles her feet. "Is it? Helping, I mean?"

Brandi turns her head sharply. "C'mon, seriously, Penny?" She flips her hair. Clearly Brandi is still upset about the Denis/Penny kiss.

"Precisely," Ann says. "How can removing the trees we tried so hard to grow be an improvement?"

"I just mean—I'm trying to understand the other side of this," Penny says.

"I don't know," I answer. "Do you remember how long it took for us all to pile into those buses, drive to the destinations, climb the mountains, scatter the grass seed everywhere and plant those seedlings, year after year?"

"Yup," Ann says. "And don't forget we went back regularly to check on them and monitor their health and growth for science class."

Brandi tilts her chin up. "We've literally birthed those trees and watched them mature over the years. Some of the very first trees we planted are the ones being cut down!" she says.

"Well. Not literally," Ann says. "We didn't give birth."

"Right." Brandi laughs awkwardly.

I put a hand on Brandi's shoulder. "It doesn't matter which trees, exactly, we planted. The point is, all the trees are important. We've all learned how badly Sudbury needs them. Now we have to fight for them."

Penny nods her head. I think she sees it our way now. I hope she does.

The bell rings.

"Well." I pause for effect. "This is it." I look them each in the eye. "Our last day together at Rockwood Public." A gust of sadness overwhelms me, even though I've been counting down for weeks. "It would have been so boring without you all." How on earth could our friendship be over by the end of the summer? It seems impossible standing here, together. But in a way, everything *is* changing. I bite down on my lip.

Penny reaches for me. "We had a lot of good times here," she says.

A football smacks Ann in the back. "I won't miss everything," she says and whips the ball back into the field. "Let's not get too sentimental, okay?" She brushes her hands on her shorts.

"Yeah," Brandi says. "What she said. I don't want to cry. Not here. I'll see you losers at lunch." She smiles with tears in her eyes.

Penny wipes at her tears and so do I, at least before I reach the set of blue doors for the very last time.

CHAPTER 24

After we empty our desks and lockers, return library books and eat way too many cupcakes made by our homeroom teacher; after we play one last game of soccer baseball, students versus teachers (we win 8–7); after we cry a little and laugh a lot and shoot down the stairs when the final bell rings and we say our final tearful goodbyes, I make my way home. I take the long way because I'm not ready for it to end just yet. I'm a high schooler now. It's amazing how fast things can shift in one day, after you wait a whole lifetime.

Once I'm home, I beeline it to my bedroom to grab my journal and my favourite pen from Poppy's lunch box. I then race downstairs and straight out the door. Summer holidays have officially begun!

For the last few days, Mom has been back to work in a big way. She's been super preoccupied, which is a good thing. She's not asking me a thousand questions about where I'm going and what I'm doing.

I'm taking my new bike to Birchwood for the first time, and with Ann not there, I'm kind of worried about how Penny and Brandi will get along. I think it's time they work things out, at least for the sake of Birchwood. We planned to meet at Kipling Park and walk up the hill together.

They both arrive from opposite sides of the road, and I don't even give them a chance to say a word before I tell them, "Let's go, we need to find out what the heck is going on up there!" We push our bikes up around the base of the mountain and walk past Birchwood. It looks smaller, even from here, like it's not possible that we could all fit inside, which is strange because it's only been a week.

"Brandi, any luck with those books to help identify the miscellaneous plants and trees?"

"Yup. Zero issues taking those books out of the library," she says with a slight chuckle. "I already started making a list of the ones I remembered. Ms. Barry was all like 'You might need this one too, Miss Adams, and might I interest you in this encyclopedia of plant life from the nineteenth century?' She said she would hold the other two books that can help us, once they are returned."

"That's great," Penny says, trying to make eye contact with Brandi.

Brandi ignores her.

I say, "It really is, but having the pictures with the plants will make our case even stronger. So, you and Penny can work together on this, right?"

"Guess so." Brandi shrugs her shoulders.

"Brandi." Penny pulls on her sleeve.

"Not now."

We keep walking until we reach the yellow tape that says NO TRESPASSING. And then I see a new sign that must have been added this week: AT YOUR OWN RISK.

"You guys, we're going to have to move faster if we hope to stop this." I tuck the pen behind my ear.

"I can't believe how different it already looks," Penny says. "Like one day it's here and the next day it's gone."

Brandi bends down to smell the large patch of wildflowers. "This makes me really blue. How can people not care about this land? There's so much life here."

"I know. This is why we need to get cracking," I answer. "Thank goodness they're not working weekends. It buys us some time."

Brandi and Penny start recording the plants and trees while I continue my work on the animals and birds. I quickly add a red-tailed hawk, a tree swallow, a northern mockingbird and many chickadees, and by the end of the afternoon, I've also added a woodpecker, a garter snake, a badger, several hopping baby frogs and one large Blanding's turtle. Thanks to last year's science class, I know that Blanding's turtles are dangerously declining every year, so I put a star beside that one.

Then I notice the trees are leaning into each other, like they're having a heartfelt conversation. I wonder what they're saying to each other? I think about my great-granddaddy and how I wish he were here to help us. Just thinking about him makes me want to work even harder to save this forest. He tried to protect the trees on his own. At least I have my three friends helping me. I want to believe the trees are happy we're here. If they can speak, like Grandma says, then just maybe they can hear us trying to save them too.

The late afternoon sun is glaring down on my face. I should have worn a hat. I circle back to the girls. They're kneeling in the long grass, scribbling in their notebooks.

"How's it going over here?" I ask, shielding my eyes from the light.

"Good. I think we added nearly all of the species we've come across. There are just a few wildflowers we're not sure about," Penny says.

I get closer. "Do you mind sharing what you have so far?"

Brandi looks at her notepad and goes through her list one by one. "So far, in TREES, I found birch, willow, white pine, red pine, poplar, spruce and maple. Oh! And cedar, too."

Penny pipes up and says, "And in WILDFLOWERS, I found bunchberry, starflower, twinflower, lily of the valley and the red baneberry, not to mention the obvious black-eyed Susans, buttercups and daisies."

"This is excellent, you guys. Let's call it for now and meet back later after Ann is done with the graduation party. We need to get the rest of the nocturnal animals before we bring this information to Mayor Sumac. I think we should give ourselves a deadline of one week, at the very most, to complete everything and present it to council. Once we have the notes, drawings and possible photos together in one binder, it will be hard for the city to deny all of the natural resources and wildlife we'll be losing."

"I'll call Ann once I get home to check in," Penny says.

"Perfect."

We climb back on our bikes and cycle down the path we know so well and up through the park. Penny keeps going but I ask Brandi to wait.

She stops super dramatically, breaking hard and making a groove in the sand. "What's with the secret meeting?" She rolls her eyes. She's been rolling her eyes a lot lately.

"Brandi, I know you're upset, but do you think you can move past this? It would make things easier, you know?"

"Easy for you to say. She doesn't like Hari. And Hari doesn't like her."

"Yeah, but you don't know how she feels. Talk to her about it," I reply, trying to make my voice extra gentle.

Brandi frowns. "It won't change what happened. Denis volunteered to kiss her and she didn't exactly say no." She takes off and zigzags across the road, then disappears around the bend.

Great. That went well.

I veer left and pedal back home to Vine Avenue. I'm not sure if Mom is home yet. I really hope she's still at work. I break hard before turning into the driveway. Roger's company truck, with *Carling King Construction* in big letters along the side, is parked behind our car.

I jump off my bike, snap my kickstand and sneak through the door as quietly as humanly possible. I slowly peer around the corner and spot Mom and Roger on the couch, kissing.

"Wolf. You're here!" Mom catches sight of me and scrambles to her feet, tucking her hair behind her ears.

"I live here, Mom."

"Of course, honey. Roger just came by to drop off some papers."

"Yup, that's the story," he says, smiling with his cheeks puffed out, hair messy.

"Where have you been?" she asks.

"Just out with my friends. Nothing illegal," I answer.

"Nothing fun, then," he says under his breath, cracking himself up. "Wolf"—he snaps his fingers—"I gotcha some beads. I saw a box of them at a yard sale. I figured you'd know what to do with them, seeing as your shoes are coated with 'em."

Another thoughtful gift? Why does he keep doing this to me?

"Thanks," I say. "That's nice of you."

"You old softy." Mom leans against him.

"It's nothing, I uh, I'll grab it from the truck and leave it by the shed before I go."

I wish he would stop surprising me like this. How can a guy who buys beads for a girl at a yard sale not care about rabbits and turtles and trees?

"Well, honey, on another note, we have dinner plans. Why don't you eat with Grandma tonight? I just called her and she's had a bout of food poisoning but she'd still love for you to come over and stay the night."

"All right," I say, relieved that I don't have to spend Friday evening watching them make eyes at each other. Besides, I haven't seen Grandma all week. It will be nice to spend time with her.

"Here's some money for pizza so she doesn't have to cook."

"Make sure you buy pizza and not beer," Roger says.

"Oh, Roger." Mom laughs and ties her high-heeled sandals.

I pack an overnight bag and ride my bike to Grandma's. I don't like to hear she's had food poisoning but maybe it'll be better that she's not her usual keen self.

I still plan to meet the girls at Birchwood after dinner.

CHAPTER 25

Welcome to girls night!" Grandma announces, as I step inside.

"Sorry to hear you're feeling sick, Grandma."

"Thank you, dear. I think it might be that fancy sushi I ate over at Mrs. Mancini's. It's always the fancy stuff you have to watch out for."

"Noted." I give her a thumbs-up.

"So, what will it be tonight? Poker? Twenty-one? Should we hit the slots? I can make you some mac and cheese à la broccoli."

"Mom gave me some money for pizza. Let's order in, so you can rest."

"Pizza it is!" But then she clutches her chest. "I think I should sit down."

"Oh, Grandma," I say, carefully taking her arm. "Let's sit and watch some TV."

"Now you're talking, Granddaughter."

I notice how pale she looks as I help her to her armchair. Maybe I ought to stay home tonight to make sure she doesn't get any worse.

"Give me the phone and let me order that pizza. Anchovies only," she says with a smirk.

"The usual please, Grandma."

"Only onions," she answers, and dials the number to Cortina Pizza.

"Grandma! Only *pepperoni*," I add with extra emphasis, just in case.

I eat two large slices of pizza and watch more TV with Grandma before she says she needs to go lie down. She didn't even touch her pizza.

"Do you need anything? I mean, can I do something to help?"

"Not a thing. Your old grandma is going to be just fine. Just an upset stomach is all. I'll be fit as a fiddle by tomorrow. Come and say goodnight."

I hug her soft body and she kisses the top of my head. "Now scram and go watch something inappropriate while I go take something to help me sleep. There's an extra pillow in that hall closet if you need it."

"I'll be fine. Thank you."

"I know." She cups my cheek.

I should be hightailing it to Birchwood. Instead, I'm cycling in front of Hari's house. There's a few cars in the driveway, probably those family members visiting for Mr. Patel's funeral. I haven't spoken to Hari since the night of my birthday and I was really hoping to see him on the last day of school, but he never came. I slow down as I reach his house. I'm secretly hoping that maybe he'll see me and come outside to talk to me. But once I see a shadow pass by the window, I totally lose my nerve and pedal like mad past his house, until I reach the top of the path through Kipling Park.

I nudge my bike up the hill, and at last, I reach the five birch trees. All three girls are already here.

"Late again," Ann says.

"I was at Grandma Houle's, so it took me a little longer to get here," I explain, but I can feel my cheeks reddening. I'm too embarrassed to tell them I was wasting time in front of Hari's.

Ann cracks a smile. "I'm just bugging you." She turns on her heels.

"Wolf, it looks like they were up here after we left," Brandi says. "They brought more equipment. You can see tractors through the trees up there."

"But how? It's been like four hours since we were here."

"I can't believe how different it already feels," Ann says. "It's now or never."

"With this destruction speeding up, we need to finish categorizing, even if it takes all night." I push back a yawn. "Are you all in?" I ask.

"All in," they answer, without wavering.

We split up in pairs and start working like bees, each focusing on our tasks. I'm walking near the base of the mountain with Ann, who's already listed and identified the pond and Junction Creek, which eventually flows into Kelly Lake in the south end of Sudbury. Our task tonight is to list the nocturnal animals, together.

There's yellow tape all along the way now, and a few yellow tractors stamped with the Carling King Construction logo on them. A crown. I think about the golden necklace and the box of beads—his acts of kindness are at war with what's in plain sight in front of me. It's like he's two different people. And that's when I spot it.

"No. No, no, no, no, no."

"What? What is it?" Ann hurries over.

I flare my mini-flashlight on the orange arrows spray-painted along the mountain.

"No way. Seriously? Forests and creeks are not enough? They want our mountain too?" Ann says.

I shake my head in disbelief. "It sure looks that way."

Brandi slaps the patch of rock with her hand. "Don't they blast them when they want to build new roads?"

"Yeah, you're right." I bite the inside of my cheeks.

Ann traces an arrow with her finger.

"Let's follow them," I tell her.

She tightens her shoelaces, and I take the lead with my flashlight and trail the line of arrows around the ridge of the mountain.

"It looks like they go up." I point. "Should we climb the mountain and follow?"

"I think we definitely should," Ann answers. "Maybe it will indicate how much of the tip they want to remove. I'm sure they'll want these houses at the top, for those views."

"Yeah, makes sense," I say, uneasiness bubbling in my stomach again. "Now we have to add a mountain to the list of lost resources. Once you blast it, you can never get it back."

"Yup. Neverville." Brandi is pacing in circles.

"I'll stay here," Penny says. "Can you stay with me, Brandi? I don't want to be alone, just in case." Her hands are joined together, begging her to stay.

"Fine," Brandi grumbles.

I tuck the flashlight in my back pocket and Ann and I start climbing the two-hundred-plus-foot mountain. I look for deep cracks to grip my feet and place my hands in. It's a steady slope, which makes it possible to climb without any special gear. Besides, we know how to climb these mountains. We've always climbed these mountains. Even so, I'm being extra careful in the growing dark. When we reach about twenty feet up from the ground, I notice a section of the mountain that's open, with a large boulder at the entrance of it. I wait for Ann to make it to the ledge and reach for her hand to help pull her up.

"What's this?" Ann says, rubbing the dirt off her pants.

"It looks like a cave." I smack the large boulder. "Do you think the earthquake created it? I don't remember it being here before. We've explored every bit of this mountain."

"It could be," Ann says.

I slide my flashlight out of my pocket and flood the inside with light. As soon as I point the light on the walls, I see pictures on them, paintings in bright red. Images of deer and moose, canoes and other symbols I don't recognize. "Oh my! This can't be real!"

Ann shuffles over and gasps. "What? But, how? This is unbelievable!" she cries.

"Ann, are you seriously seeing what I'm seeing?"

"What is it?" Brandi shouts from below. "What is it?"

I turn and look back down to the ground and let my eyes adjust to the dark. I'm trying to steady myself by holding onto the edge of the rock when my flashlight slips from my hand and crashes to the bottom of the cavern.

"Just great!" I stick my head deeper into the cave.

"Be careful!" Ann says. "Don't fall in!"

Penny shrieks from below. "Tell us! Please! What do you see?"

"You guys, I think there are pictographs in here!" I holler back.

"Yeah, it looks like REAL ancient pictographs." Ann's echo drums within the cave.

The light from my flashlight is still beaming, even though it fell; it's casting a glow against the red outlines of the bulls and deer, moose and arrows. "There must be at least fifty drawings, or more," I say, with utter astonishment.

Ann scooches closer to me. "It's like I've stepped into one of my books," she says.

"Is it just me or does it *feel* special in here, like my arms have major truth bumps but I'm not cold whatsoever."

"Totally. It feels positively extraordinary. And—oh my goodness—this is just what we needed! They cannot destroy this. Not with this treasure inside. It's a cultural artifact," Ann says, in the most solemn voice I've ever heard before.

"Absofreakinglutely. Drawings like this are sacred. Grandma Houle told me about them when I was little. She used to take a canoe to see some with her dad along the Ottawa River."

Ann leans her head inside the cave a little more. "What about the flashlight? Should we try to get it?" she asks.

I check my Swatch. "I want to, but it's getting late and I'm staying at Grandma's tonight. Plus, we should still finish our cataloguing."

"That's true," she says, her voice now tense.

"You know, maybe if they see the flashlight beam, they'll find the pictographs too, and then they'll want to protect them, like we do."

"Let's hope so," she says.

I peer inside one last time and my arms erupt with truth bumps again. I can't believe this treasure we found. It feels so incredibly special—I feel it all the way inside my bones. Deeper even.

"Wait, what's that?" Ann points to a shiny something hiding in the crack of the mountain past my feet.

She reaches over and grabs a metal tape measure with the Carling King Construction logo on it. "Looks like someone was standing right where we are," she says.

"Does that mean they know about them?" I ask.

"Maybe they just found them, like us. That's probably why they halted the work."

"Yeah, that's true. I really hope so, Ann."

"They're probably just as flabbergasted as we are by this rare finding."

"Maybe they're trying to find people to help them figure out what to do and how to protect them."

"Exactly."

I climb back down the mountain and jump the last few feet, leaning into Brandi and Penny to break my fall.

"Brandi! Penny! It's unbelievable!" My arms are swinging in the air.

Brandi jumps on the spot. "What do they look like?"

"Animal line drawings painted in red," I tell her.

Ann lands on the ground. "It's a red ochre, most likely a mineral mixed with animal oil. Pictographs can be white, black or red. I think red are the prettiest, though," she says.

Penny is on the tips of her toes. "But what kind of drawings were there?"

"All kinds! Canoes, deer, even triangles!" I tell her. "I seriously cannot believe it."

"Serpents and thunderbirds, too," Ann continues. "Due to our location, these are most likely Ojibway or Algonquin, possibly Odawa. Some of the pictographs found across the Canadian Shield are two thousand years old!"

"How do you know all of this?" Brandi asks, touching the side of the mountain with her palm.

"I like to read. You know this."

"Well, I read too, but, you know, Sweet Valley High," Brandi says.

"I don't judge." Ann snort-laughs and sucks it back in.

We all start to laugh at Ann's laugh, and then because Ann *is* judging and we all know it, we just keep laughing. Probably because we're tired and we're also equally excited and feeling completely overwhelmed by this extraordinary discovery. We can't stop cackling and snorting. The giggle-fest continues until we're all holding our bellies from cramping pain.

When we finally catch our breath, Ann says, "Girls, we finally have what it takes to save this place. There's no way the city will let them build here now."

"So what's the plan? Who do we tell about the pictographs so that the construction will stop?" Penny asks.

I look at Ann. "Actually, we think they know about them already. We found a measuring tape up there."

"Oh. So they found the pictographs, like us?" Penny says. "Maybe that's why the arrows point upward."

"Maybe." Ann zips up her sweater.

"Either way, I still think we should put all our cataloguing information together, along with a description of the picto-graphs, and present it to the council like we planned."

Ann puts her hand on my shoulder. "You know, it's no wonder Birchwood has always felt so sacred to us," she says.

"Positively." I say with a hand over my heart. "This is an ancient sacred site. People have gathered here in harmony with nature for centuries. Just like us."

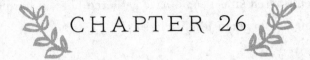

CHAPTER 26

We decide to work through the night to finish our cataloguing so we have a complete report to submit to the council on Monday. The sun is cresting with peaches and pinks staining the bottom of the sky. My head feels funny and my body is weak. I'm also feeling super guilty about being out all night, even though it was for a very good cause. I hope Grandma slept right through.

"Okay, we should get back before the sun rises and we get busted for not being in our beds. Let's meet up later today," I tell them.

Ann tightens her ponytail. "Say nothing to no one until we have the plan all figured out."

"Do you think it's time we tell our parents, though?" Penny asks. "This seems like a really big deal."

"You might be right," Brandi says, surprisingly agreeing with her.

"Yeah," I say. "Let's regroup and decide once we get some rest."

We get on our bikes to return home. Everyone is in their own separate world as we ride down the path. I wave goodbye and pedal to Grandma's house. The sky is glowing. There's barely any trace of night hanging above.

I'm exhausted but I'm also feeling lit from within. I still can't believe we found pictographs! Inside *our* mountain. A real buried treasure. What would Grandma say about this? I suddenly want to tell her everything. We need an ally. Someone who understands how important these pictographs are. I hope the pack will agree that she's a grown-up we can trust.

I sneak in through the back window and notice the bedroom door is wide open, which means that Grandma knows I was gone. I tiptoe into the kitchen and step back when I see Mrs. Lehtinen, Grandma's neighbour, sitting at the table holding a cup of coffee in her hands.

"There you are, young lady. Where have you been?" She leaves her steaming mug on the table.

"Where's my grandma?"

"Your grandma is at the hospital. She called an ambulance this morning to take her in."

My whole body suddenly feels numb.

"An ambulance? What happened?"

"Wolf, I'm going to let your mother deal with this. She's coming over right now. I called her immediately when I realized you weren't in that bed," she says, one hand pointing to the room and one on her small hip.

"B-but . . ." I stutter. "Is my grandma okay?" I ask, my lips quivering.

Mrs. Lehtinen softens. "She's okay. She's getting tests done at the hospital. That's all I can tell you right now. Let me make you something to eat. But go and wash your hands first."

I head to the bathroom and start soaping my hands and the tears gush from my tired eyes. I should have been here. I feel so horrible. I stagger out and sit at the kitchen table.

A cool breeze reaches me as Mom storms through the door.

"Mom! I'm sorry!" I leap to my feet.

"Wolf! We're going to have a serious talk about this, but right now I want you to grab your things. We're going to the hospital."

I glimpse Roger through the window in his Trans Am, engine on, waiting in the driveway.

"Thank Mrs. Lehtinen," Mom says.

"Um, thank you, Mrs. Lehtinen." I can feel her disapproving eyes in her heavy, knitted forehead staring down on me, scorching through my skin. I totally deserve it. "I'm sorry," I say, trying not to sob.

"You listen to your mother now."

Mom ushers me out the door and we step into the early light. The birds are chirping happily, like everything is perfectly fine.

"Wolf! What were you thinking?" Mom charges for the car and waits for me to climb in the back seat. She slams the door. "You knew your grandmother was ill."

"I know." I buckle my seatbelt. "I feel terrible." My voice quivers and my heart thumps through my chest.

She cranes her neck to look at me. "Listen, I know you're upset about Grandma and so am I, so we'll hold off on talking about this right now. But we are definitely going to talk about this sneaking-out business later."

"I know." I fold my arms and lower my eyes.

"All right." She pats my arm before she faces the front again. "Let's go."

I watch Roger in the rear-view mirror. He's completely silent, focused on the road.

I try to keep my tears from falling, but I don't think I can.

CHAPTER 27

Now I'm dizzy from not sleeping all night and I'm nauseous with worry. Using the wall for balance, I slide along the hallway: white walls, white floors and bright, blinding lights. After a few doors, I can hear Grandma in her emergency room, talking to someone.

"That's the way it goes sometimes, toots!" Despite feeling queasy, I sprint towards her voice, into room 142, and throw myself in her arms.

"Hey now, Granddaughter, what is happening here?" she says, with both her arms wrapped around me.

"I'm sorry I wasn't there. I'm sorry you needed me and I wasn't there. That will never ever happen again. I promise. I promise. Cross my heart and hope to die." Tears plummet as I gasp for air.

"Hey now. Shhh. Shhh. Sometimes a girl's got to sneak out of the house every once in a while. God knows, I did. Maybe not your mom," she whispers in my ear, "but this old girl understands." She sweeps my bangs off my face, wiping my cheeks with her gentle and creased hands. Grandma pulls me in and hugs me hard. She kisses the top of my head, and my whole world is starting to feel right again.

"I'll be back soon to draw some blood, Mrs. Houle," the nurse says before leaving the room.

"Goodie, I can't wait." Grandma rubs my back. I manage to slow my breath, in and out, in and out. From behind me I hear my mom and Roger come in.

"Now, what do we have here, Daughter? A visitor of the male persuasion?"

Mom takes Roger's hand. "Mother, this is Roger. Roger Carling. The man I told you about."

"Pleasure to meet you, ma'am, I mean not under these circumstances, but a pleasure, still." He clears his throat and steps forward awkwardly to shake her hand, barely gripping the tips of her fingers.

"Well, I'm not dead, so these are as good as any," Grandma says.

I can tell she's not sure about him.

Mom steps forward, away from Roger. "Mother, how are you feeling? Was it the food poisoning?"

Grandma sighs. "Well, no. Not exactly. It's not food poisoning, Cathy."

"It's not?"

"Nope." She sighs once more. "It never was." Grandma closes her eyes.

"Mother, what is going on?"

I sit up and look at Grandma, my heart pauses with my breath.

"Nothing that doesn't happen to other folks, I guess." Grandma straightens the blankets over her legs.

"Mother?"

"Grandma?"

"Girls."

Mom's face drains of any colour. She's wearing her serious business face. "Tell me. Tell me now," she says.

"Well then, there's no sense in sugar-coating this. I've got the big C." Grandma's eyes look like pools of dark glass.

"The big C?" I ask, confused.

"Cancer," Roger mumbles, loud enough for us to hear.

"Bingo, Roger! You clever guy, you." She points to him. "I didn't want to worry you."

Mom covers her mouth.

I bury my head in Grandma's chest, binding my arms around her so tight, until I can't feel my hands and fingers and the tears start falling again. Poppy was sick for a long while before they eventually found his cancer. Maybe they found it faster in Grandma. Maybe it will be different for her. I squeeze my eyes shut and open them again.

"Now, now. It will be fine." Grandma wipes her eyes with her sleeve. "I'll live a long while yet. Old people die eventually.

It turns out now I just know what will take me to the all-night party in the sky."

Mom leans against the wall and stares out the window. "What type?" she asks, her voice cracking.

"Lung cancer, dear. Good old cigars and cigarettes. Maybe there's truth to what some folks are saying about those darned things. I stopped smoking them years ago, but Poppy, well, you know he always liked his pipe. No matter, anyway."

Mom begins to cry and then I cry even more, and then Roger excuses himself from the room. "Pardon me, going to find a restroom. Too much coffee this morning. My apologies."

Mom waves him away and walks towards Grandma and me. She envelops us both in her arms, which are like two large wings, and we stay like that for a long, long while. All three of us weep until every tissue from the tissue box is soaked with our tears.

Less than fifteen minutes later, while we're both still sitting on Grandma's bed, I hear footfalls coming. It's not the nurse. It's Roger, waltzing in with three bouquets of flowers: one for Grandma, one for Mom and one for me.

CHAPTER 28

The ride home is quiet. No one says a single word. Once we arrive, I march to my bedroom and close the door behind me while Mom and Roger talk in the kitchen. I grab my journal—the one with the four of us on it: the wolf, the fox, the deer and the rabbit—and some pens and smelly markers. I haul it all into my bag and hurtle downstairs. I need to get out of here and see my friends. I tell Mom that I'm going to Brandi's place (most privacy) and, surprisingly, she lets me go, even after sneaking out. It's obvious she's distracted by what's happening with Grandma.

"Make sure you are home *before* dinner," she says while I'm lacing up my shoes. "I mean it," she adds.

"I promise," I reply and slip away, out the door before she changes her mind. I jump on my bike and cycle through the warm rain, down the paved road. I feel so dizzy and tired, but I don't stop.

I knock on the door of Brandi's two-storey house. It has orange brick with a blue door and a black metal knocker. I can see her cat Stompin' Tom in the side window.

Brandi's dad opens the door and winks.

"Well, hello there, Miss Lagacé. I wonder who you're looking for?"

He's wearing midnight-blue pants and a matching shirt, with steel-toe boots. I spot the metal lunch box by the door.

"Is Brandi home?" I ask in a scratchy voice.

"She must be, since she's not out with you," he says with a kind smile.

I force a friendly smile.

"Everything okay this morning?"

I push my shoulders back. "Yeah," I say. "Girl stuff."

He points to Brandi's downstairs bedroom. I kick off my shoes and head straight down.

This is where we hang out in the winter, when we can't get to Birchwood.

I knock on the door and fall into Brandi's arms as soon as she opens it.

"Wolf, what's wrong?"

The waterworks fall hard and fast and I've told her everything by the time we reach her daybed. Her boy-band posters listen in while I pour my heart out.

"Oh my goodness! I'm so sorry. I know how close you are. You haven't slept, have you? Why don't you try to sleep for a while in my room? I'll get us some snacks and call the others, and we'll meet here when you have rested a little."

"Okay," I say, "but actually, can we go to Birchwood instead? It's the only place I want to be right now."

"Definitely," Brandi says.

Brandi packs a blanket from her bed into a backpack and she bikes to Birchwood with me. Once we arrive, she tucks me in and tells me she'll be back in a little while with the pack.

It doesn't take long before I plunge into a deep sleep under the five birch trees, while the leaves rustle in the soft summer rain.

I open my eyes and I can see the light coming through the planks of wood and pouring through the small window in the roof. Within seconds, everything comes flooding back: Grandma, Roger, the pictographs, even Hari and his dad. I check my purple Swatch and realize that I slept for three solid hours. It's one in the afternoon and I hear the girls approaching on their bikes. They're chatting and laughing, like nothing bad is happening. I slide open the door and Ann ducks through with a small picnic basket in her hands.

Brandi and Penny are both clasping brown paper bags from Ted's Confectionary.

Brain food.

Heart food.

Food for survival.

Penny gives me a big hug. "How are you feeling? Brandi told us everything."

"Better. Well, not really. But I'm glad you're all here."

"So are we," she says.

"Do you mind if we only talk about Birchwood right now?"

Ann sits across from me. "Of course not," she says.

"Good."

"So what's our plan of action?" Penny leans in close beside me.

"Well, I was going to suggest that we tell Grandma Houle. I know she would have been able to help us." I bite my top lip hard to stop my voice from shaking. "But now . . ."

"We understand," Brandi says. "Let's think. Who else can we trust?" She hands out the snacks.

"We need someone who is knowledgeable, someone who can help us with research. And someone who knows the ins and outs of the way this city works, too," I say.

"Can your mom help us, Ann?" Penny asks. "She would know a lot of this stuff, working for the mayor."

"Actually, I don't think she's the right person. She's been really stressed out lately, and hardly ever home. Do we have any other options?"

"What about your mom, Wolf? Or Roger?" Brandi says.

I think for a really long minute. "Maybe," I finally answer. "I'm just worried about taking the chance . . . I think we should find someone on the outside of this. Just to be sure." I think for another minute. "You might not like this, but I might have the perfect person to help us." I chew on a wedge of peanut butter and jam sandwich, while I choose my words carefully.

"Who?" they ask me, all at the same time.

"Ms. Barry."

"The battleaxe?" Brandi shrieks.

Penny falls back against the pillows. "No way!"

"Are you kidding? You're kidding, right?" Ann asks.

"Wolf. Be serious," Brandi says.

"I am. Think about it. She has access to all of the city files. She's the gatekeeper to everything that has ever happened in this town. She was probably alive when the city was founded like a hundred years ago. And, I think, deep inside, she's a good person." My voice cracks. "I think it's worth a try."

Ann's quiet for a few long seconds before she says, "She did put those books aside for us."

"And she helped me identify a bunch of those wildflowers," Brandi says.

"And," I add, "she cares deeply about nature *and* history."

Penny pops a red licorice foot in her mouth. "Okay, so would we tell her everything?" she asks, with a bucket of doubt in her voice.

"Everything," I answer. "She knows about rules and process. She'll know who to talk to and where to go."

Ann is in deep thought. I can see her brain at work as she rests her chin on her knee. "I can't believe I'm saying this, but I think you're right." She nods her head in approval. "Ms. Barry's very passionate about history and anything ancient, really."

Penny nibbles on a green apple wedge. "It's still a huge risk, though, I mean if Roger doesn't do the right thing."

"Yeah," Brandi says, "and look what happened with Ms. Jeffries when we asked her for help. Aren't adults supposed to be the ones who know better?"

"And do better," Ann says.

"I know. That was really disappointing. But we're running out of time and options, and desperate times call for desperate measures," I answer. Penny puts an arm around my back, and in that moment, it's decided. We'll ask Ms. Barry, the ancient library gatekeeper, to help us save our sacred woods *and* the pictographs from destruction.

"She does worship plants," Brandi giggles.

"Major understatement!" says Ann. "When should we talk to her?"

"Now." I get up from the pile of pillows, and the blanket slips off my legs.

"May I suggest we go after this buffet of peanut butter and jam sandwiches, apple wedges and assorted candy, please?" Brandi motions her arms, like she's Vanna White.

"Of course." I crack a smile for the first time since the whole world flipped upside down, since learning about my grandma being sick.

"Penny, um, do you think we can talk outside before we go?" Brandi asks, tugging on her bracelets.

"Absolutely," Penny says with bright eyes.

This makes me smile for a second time.

CHAPTER 29

After Brandi and Penny make up and hug it out for like ten minutes and promise to never let a boy get between them again—"pinky swear, cross my heart"— we bike over to the library. There aren't many cars parked out front. It's too beautiful a day to sit inside. But this is good news for us. Less people means fewer distractions and hungry ears.

Ms. Barry is behind the desk like she always is. She's gluing paper pockets inside new books.

"Ms. Barry, hello." Oh my gosh. Did I just curtsey?

"Ms. Lagacé," she says, still gluing, not even looking up or slowing down.

"Yes. Hello. Well—" My words are all jumbled in my head. She always has a strange effect on me.

She puts down the glue bottle, weaves her hands together and peers directly at me. Her eyes are green with tiny flecks of black, like a cat's.

"Today, Ms. Lagacé." She pushes her narrow glasses up against the bridge of her pointy nose.

"We need your help!" I exclaim.

"Keep your voice *dooooown*," she loud-whispers, her long finger pressed on her lips. "Keep going," Ann utters from behind me. Brandi taps me on the back to continue.

I timidly put my hands on the table, lean in slightly and articulate clearly. "We found something in the forest and we need your help," I finally say.

"I don't have time for mischief. I have piles of work to complete, young lady."

"It's important, Ms. Barry, and it's time-sensitive. Can we talk to you in private, please?" I add, along with a bob.

"Well, this better be categorically necessary," she says.

"We'll be quick about it."

"Just you." She points to me. "Follow me."

We disappear into the far room, the dark room where all the old, dusty books go to expire, or at least get boxed up for the next community book sale. As soon as Ms. Barry clicks the door shut, I tell her everything. My hands are moving up and down and all around, and Ms. Barry goes from arms tightly crossed and lips pointed to eyes wide-open and bulging, with both hands flat against her mouth. She paces up and down the aisle a couple of times, scratching her temples, her hands dancing from forehead to chin and across her heart before she rushes for the door, leaving me to catch up. Her white runners slap against the grey linoleum tile as she dashes right past the pack.

"Let's go, girls!" she says. "And hustle!"

"Where are we going?" Brandi asks.

"On an operation. Make sure your laces are tied." She points to Brandi's shoe. "We need to boogie."

Ms. Barry breaks her number-one rule and raises her voice in the library. "Ms. French, please take over the front desk. I have an emergency!" She doesn't even wait for a response before whipping off her name tag and tossing it on the counter.

❧

We're all in line now, riding our bicycles and following Ms. Barry, who is leading. She has a yellow bike with a wide seat and a giant white wicker basket. She's leaning forward with her head nearly touching the handlebars and her legs are making enormous circles. We turn the corner onto Beatrice Crescent and she flies off her bike like a gymnast, which is really surprising considering her age. She's not as old as Grandma, but close.

"Give me five minutes." She disappears into the house.

"This situation feels very bizarre." Brandi straddles her bike.

"I can't believe we're at Ms. Barry's place," Penny says. "Remember when we tried to call her?"

"I can't believe she even lives in a regular house." Ann looks around. "I thought she might live in a greenhouse or something."

"Or a giant mushroom," I say. We all laugh, but not in a mean way. I can tell we're relieved to finally have someone helping us. Two minutes later, her front door swings open and she's ditched her two-piece suit for something we were never ever expecting. She's wearing military camouflage pants and an olive-green T-shirt with *2912 Cadet Army Corps* written across it. She looks like a completely different person.

"Oh my goodness, Ms. Barry has flipped her lid," Brandi mutters behind her hand.

"Are those high-tops?" Penny asks.

Ann's glowing with pure delight. "Yup."

"High-tops AND military camo?" Brandi covers her eyes in disbelief.

"Yup," Ann says again, now smiling from ear to ear. "I heard she was a civilian army cadet officer, back in the day," she whispers. "I just didn't believe it."

Brandi gives her a thumbs-up. "You look pretty fly, Ms. B."

"Takes one to know one." She makes a half twirl in each direction.

"We really underestimated her," I mumble under my breath.

Ms. Barry steps forward. "Fall in." We create a huddle. "What you have been doing is very commendable," she says. "We need to protect those pictographs. Those sacred stories cannot be replaced. You did the right thing to ask for help. I'd like to believe that the construction company will be halting their progress if they know about this, but it's too risky not to share the information with the police and our local elders.

Let's head up there so you can show me this treasure. I packed my camera in my backpack"—she points to it over her shoulder—"that way I can document it. We will then rendez-vous with the authorities before it's too late."

I'm so happy to hear Ms. Barry's words. We don't have to carry this major secret alone anymore. We have help. She was definitely the right pick.

We climb back onto our bikes, and now I'm leading the way with Ms. Barry at the end of our line. I feel hopeful again. I know we're on the right side of this and it feels really good to be moving forward. Even the flowers look happy as I ride past them. Their bellies are open and kissing the bright blue sky. I try to communicate with a striking row of dark green pine trees as we zoom past them. I can smell their sharp and refreshing needles. I hope they can hear what's in my mind and deep inside my heart. *Tell your friends we're coming to save them. We won't let them hurt you anymore. Help is coming! Pass it on!* I breathe in their fresh scent, and while I don't hear anything back, the birds are chirping loudly and the wind is whistling in my ears.

Five minutes later, a white car comes rushing towards us, traversing the road. I grip my handlebars and hear Ms. Barry holler, "Hold up, troop, stand down."

We all break on the spot, while the car screeches to a stop. It slams in reverse and breaks again abruptly, making an awful noise.

"There you are, Sheila!" the woman in the car says.

I seriously never thought of Ms. Barry having a first name before. It's a shock to hear it.

"I've been trying to reach you. I even tried the CB radio."

"Flo, I'm on a mission here. I left it behind."

"Well, listen up." She leans out of her window. "Farmer Johnson has been trying to get ahold of you. I don't want you to panic, but your bees are swarming. Bob said that they're moving towards the Boys and Girls Club, and they've got a few dozen campers out that way."

"Oh no!" Ms. Barry looks positively panicked. "They're unpredictable when they're swarming." Ms. Barry glances at her watch. She's scratching her head. "I'm sorry," she says, "but I have to attend to my bees before I can assist you. I'll find you. I'm a certified tracker. You can count on me, girls."

She salutes us and hops back on her bike and starts racing down the road, following the white Volkswagen bug.

I stand there watching her get smaller and smaller until she disappears. Everything is suddenly so quiet, it's almost eerie.

Penny sits down on the ground beside her bike. "Why can't anything go right?"

"She'll be back. I know she'll meet us there." Ann stares at the empty road.

"I hope so," I say.

🍂

We make our way to the mountain. As we approach the area, we notice more signs have been added along the path, to keep people away. We hear trucks backing out and beeps sounding off.

"Get down," I say. "Stay low."

We all crouch down and suck in our breath.

"Let's hide our bikes in here," Brandi murmurs and points to a large bush full of foliage.

"I count five men, and three of them look hefty but the other two look like the athletic type. I think they could definitely catch us if we had to dart for cover," I whisper.

"I'm worried." Penny's voice quivers. "They're not supposed to be working on the weekend and it's Saturday."

Ann straightens her glasses and whispers. "I guess this means they didn't decide to stop construction because they found the pictographs. So now what?"

"Someone's coming," I say as my heart hiccups.

"Get down. Cover yourself," Brandi peeps.

I pull two branches with dark green leaves over my head and freeze like a statue. I try not to move a single inch.

"I'll take care of it, Roger."

"Thanks, Jim. You're the best foreman I've ever had."

"It's no trouble."

"We need to stay on schedule if we want to keep those guys in Toronto happy. Our backers will move on if this development is delayed for any reason. We can't let anything stop us from moving forward. The future of this town is riding on this one," Roger says.

I can see him through the branches of the thick pine. He looks worried. Agitated. Don't move, Wolf. Don't freaking breathe. I pinch my eyes shut.

"I'm on it, boss," Jim answers.

"All right. Keep me posted," Roger says.

Thankfully, he walks away and we let out a collective sigh of relief.

After they are completely out of sight, and we make sure no other worker is coming from the site, we make a plan: Ann and I will climb the mountain again and draw the pictographs as a backup. Once Ms. Barry arrives, she can take the photos and we'll add the film to our list of proof. Then, we'll take the notes, film, drawings and everything else we know to the North Regional Police Station. And we'll tell our parents. We can't risk any more delays.

We'll save this mountain from the king of destruction and his lovesick queen.

CHAPTER 30

We wait another hour before the machines stop beeping and the men leave. We quickly set our plan in motion. Brandi and Penny are on the lookout for anybody coming back. They'll make a crow call to warn us of any trespassers. I'll climb the mountain with Ann and we'll draw each pictograph as best as we can.

"Hurry, Ann, let's go," I say.

"I'm right behind you."

"Be careful," Brandi says and puts an arm around Penny's shoulder.

Ann and I reach the large boulder in record time. My heart is pounding and my hands are a little shaky as I approach the opening of the mountain again. I brace myself before I look in, and I'm so relieved when I still see the pictographs there, with the late-afternoon sun spilling inside the cave.

"Oh, they're even more beautiful than the last time," Ann says.

"They really are!" I have shivers just looking at them.

"Let's both draw them," Ann says. "Just in case we miss one."

"Good idea."

I sit up on my knees, while Ann sits with her legs crossed. We begin to sketch the pictographs right away. I follow each red line with my eyes, slowly moving the pencil along on the page. I'm mostly looking at the image, only glancing down to make sure I got it right. I start with the two small triangles and then a deer with antlers and something that looks like a beaver to me. I skip a couple of lines I can't make out and then begin again with the canoe and some squiggly lines that look like they are moving on the wall. The whole time I'm drawing, I can't help but feel super fortunate for being able to witness these. I start drawing a little faster because I want to save these pictographs more than anything. Everyone should have a chance to see them.

I wonder what my great-granddaddy would say about this? I'm positive he would want me to do everything I can to save them. I'm so curious what these pictographs might mean. I want to learn so much more about my Algonquin heritage and the Ojibway too. I really want to learn what these painted stories represent.

I count each image in my journal and the ones on the wall. I calculate forty-six images in all. I glance over at Ann, who is utterly laser-focused, drawing the final image.

"There," Ann says and then sighs. "Finding these pictographs is the best thing that's ever happened to me."

"I feel the exact same way. Now let's get down from here so we can save them."

As we descend, the sky is streaked with deep violet, and the sun is blood orange as it begins to sink behind the mountain. Nature really is the best painting ever. When my feet touch the ground, I start to feel super tired and hungry.

"Did you get them all?" Brandi asks.

"Every single one," I say.

Penny pats my arm. "Good job, you two. But, still no Ms. Barry," she says, pouting. "I wonder if she got lost?"

"I doubt it," Ann says.

The sun flickers through the leaves and catches my attention. I wonder if the trees up here recognize us because we've been here so often.

Ann places her notebook in her basket and flicks up her kickstand. "We should go."

"Yeah, but should we bike over to Ms. Barry's again?" Brandi asks.

"In the morning," I say. "Let's not get in trouble now."

Brandi drags her bicycle out of the bushes and kicks the twigs out of her spokes. "Are you coming, Wolf?"

"Yeah, I just want to double-check that we haven't forgotten anything." I also have this urge to stay among the trees for a few minutes. Ever since that hike with Grandma, I feel like I'm looking at trees in a different way.

"Wolf, what are you going to do about Roger and your mom?" Penny asks. Roger was here. It seems pretty likely he knows about the pictographs and he's just ignoring them.

"I'm not sure yet." I dig my heels in the ground. "Roger must know. But I don't know if my mom does."

"So, will you tell her, then?" Brandi says.

"Soon."

"Well, I need to get home. Don't stay too long." Brandi starts pedalling.

"I won't," I answer.

"Bye, Wolf." Penny and Ann both wave.

I take one last walk around the grounds to make sure we covered up our tracks. The warm summer breeze is whirling through the trees. Crows are cawing and the bullfrogs are crooning too. There's so much life here, so much life amid this mountain filled with ancient stories. I can't help but feel proud that we're trying to save it. I walk over to a birch tree and place my hand on it. I close my eyes and breathe in deeply. I speak to it without words, and talk from my heart, like Grandma told me. *I hope you know how much we care about you, and how grateful we are that you are here.* I feel a little silly, but I try again. *I want you to know that we will do everything we can to save you and your family—*

I'm straining my ears so much to hear something back from the tree that I startle when I hear a branch snap nearby. I scurry to the trail and drag my bike out from the bushes, and then I smell cigarette smoke. When I turn the corner and grip both handlebars—I see Roger. He's staring right at me and there's nowhere to hide. I can't even get around him because the path is so narrow. I freeze.

"Wolf, what in the bananas are you doing out here?" He looks surprised to see me. "Does your mother know you're out wandering the woods like this?" He spits on the ground.

"I'm not wandering."

"You lost, then?" He wrinkles his forehead.

"I was just looking for berries. Raspberries, actually. Ann told me I could find some out here."

"At this hour?" He moves in closer to me. "Ain't no berries here, little Wolf. Now get on home." He takes a step closer. "I mean it. It's dangerous out here," he says in a deep, booming voice. "Didn't you see the signs?" He points to the warnings up the path.

"I saw them. I see everything," I say, trying to stand up straighter.

"Well, you gotta be careful. There's wild animals out here. You could easily get hurt in a place like this," he says.

I'm as still and silent as a stone.

"I don't want to see you so close to the construction line again, you hear?" He tosses his cigarette on the ground and crushes it with his boot.

"I hear you loud and clear," I say, trying my hardest to keep my voice from trembling. I climb on my bike and pedal down the hill, as fast as I can. My heart is racing, like Tour de France fast, but it's not because I'm going fast. I'm scared. Ten out of ten scared.

While I'm propelling down at top speed, I keep asking myself the question that's spinning in my head: Did Roger warn me because he wants me to stay away from the danger or from the pictographs?

What I one hundred percent know is that he doesn't want me there whatsoever, no matter what.

CHAPTER 31

I might have broken a record, cycling back home. After parking my bike in the shed and fumbling with my lock, I rush to the side door.

"Wolf," Mom says when I burst through the door and dead-bolt it behind me. "Get over here!" She waves at me, holding the phone in the crook of her neck. My heart is still rushing. My hands are shaking. I look over my shoulder to make sure he didn't follow me. The door is still closed. Still locked.

"Grandma wants to talk to you." Mom points to the receiver. "Why on earth are you so filthy?" she asks. "Have you been rolling around in dirt all day?"

"Um. Well. Something like that." I take off my shoes and grab the phone from her, trying to slow my breath.

"You better get in the shower when you're done with that call." She hands me the phone. I bring the receiver to my ear. "Hello?"

"Granddaughter."

"Grandma." I exhale, so relieved to hear her voice.

"What were you up to? Something untoward I hope."

"How are you feeling?" I change the subject.

"Marvellous, young lady. They have me on all these pills so I'm not feeling any pain at the moment. It's like a holiday. But my brain does feel a little muddled."

"Well, that's kind of good, I guess." My heart cramps.

"Listen, are you sure everything is fine out there? You in any kind of trouble?"

"No. Why?" I glance at the front door again, and then I just start. "Grandma, I, um, I actually found something. Something incredible," I whisper. "But I'll tell you more about it when you're feeling better." I look behind me at Mom, who's washing the dishes.

"Well, you sure got me all curious. I'll wait with great enthusiasm to learn your special news."

"Okay. Great. Thanks." My heart feels right again.

"Back to my reason for calling, dear. You see, I had a strange dream and you were in it. You were running through the woods and you were terribly scared. There was a bear after you, a very large beast of a black bear, the really mean kind, so I just want you to be careful, okay? I know how you girls like to go into the woodlands and I just want you to be extra cautious, okay? I was second-guessing myself about telling you because I thought it might be the darn pills making me dream these things, but I thought I'd mention it, just in case. Can you please promise your old grandma that you'll be extra vigilant in the woods, or anywhere else for that matter?"

I'm frozen in place.

"Wolf? You still there?"

"Uh-huh. I am, Grandma. I'll be careful." I swallow hard. "Promise."

"That's my girl! Thank you for telling your grandma exactly what she wants to hear."

"No problem."

"Now go take your bath, I heard your mom say you were filthy. And thank goodness for that. You gotta live life to the fullest. It's good to get your hands full of dirt."

"I know." I swallow another hefty lump in my throat.

"Goodnight, love."

"Goodnight," I utter, barely saying it at all because the tears prick my eyes and I want to run upstairs, away from everyone and everything.

"Wolf?" Mom calls out to me. But I keep skyrocketing upstairs to run a hot bath. I plan on using half a bottle of bubble bath to wash the dirt off my skin as well as the memory of fuming Roger, who might just be the frightening furry beast in the woods.

CHAPTER 32

The golden sun gleams through my curtains. I must have slept in. I roll over and hear it again—voices in the kitchen. Laughter. What the—? I bounce out of bed and rush to my window, and there it is—Roger's company truck parked behind Mom's K-car.

I brush my teeth and get dressed in seconds. Short hair really is great when you're in a hurry. You barely have to comb it. I grab my backpack with the pictograph drawings tucked inside, sneak down the steps and listen in on their conversation.

"Is your little princess still sleeping?"

"Sure is. She's a true teenager," Mom says.

"She giving you any trouble?"

"Not my Wolf."

"Good to hear," he says. "We need to stay focused to complete the Northwood Heights development."

"I know. Things are coming along so well."

"Thanks to you. We make the best team, don't we?"

"Roger!" Mom squeals as he grabs her from behind for a kiss. "I don't want to burn these eggs."

I clear my throat like five times before entering the kitchen so I don't have to walk in on their lip-smacking. Mom steps away from Roger, tightens the pink chiffon scarf around her neck and tucks her bobby pins in place.

"Good morning, sweetheart."

"Morning."

"Slept well?"

"Like a baby." I try not to make eye contact with Roger.

"Roger came over for some coffee this morning. We need to prepare for a meeting with the city."

"A new development?" I ask.

"Yes," Mom says. "The best one yet, but I've been meaning to talk to you about it," she adds, her voice dipping.

"Let's not bore the child with business talk, Cathy," Roger says.

But Mom keeps going, her heels clicking against the floor as she walks over to the sink. "The good news is we've secured financial backing from a large company in Toronto. They see so much potential in this city. If we do well with this project, we can acquire funding for future subdivisions." Mom brims with excitement again.

Roger shifts on the stool. "Cathy, please, leave the child alone. Let's not bother her with all this."

"Okay, maybe you're right. We can talk later. What are you up to today, anyway?"

"The usual shenanigans." I force a smile.

"Well, check in on your grandma. I'm sure she'd like that now that she's settled at home again."

"She's home! That's great news. I'll stop by for sure." I grab a buttered toast from the small pile.

"What about some eggs?" she says.

"Running late this morning, Mom."

"Enjoy your day, Wolf," Roger says. "Listen to your mother and stay out of trouble."

"You know me. Always on a mission," I answer, meeting his eye. I bite into my toast and head straight for the shed to get my bike.

"See you later, honey," Mom calls after me. "And let's have a chat later this evening."

I guess my mom and I both have important things to share with each other. I know I can't delay my news for much longer. I spot the girls in the field, across the street from Ms. Barry's.

"I didn't sleep a wink last night," Penny says as I pull up. Her hair looks knotted and messy.

"Me either," Ann replies. "I stared at my ceiling all night. What about you, Wolf?"

"I slept, but it's been an interesting evening AND morning. There's been a development."

"What do you mean?" Brandi asks. I see she's added more bracelets to the collection on her arms. It's halfway to her elbow now.

"I saw Roger after you left yesterday. I stuck around to do one last walk about and he saw me on the trail. He was *not* happy—angry—actually. He warned me to stay away. Told me it was dangerous."

"No way!" Brandi says.

Penny asks, "Did he threaten you?"

"No, but I think he definitely wanted to frighten me. He flat-out told me to stay away. It was a warning, for sure."

"But maybe he's just trying to protect you? From the danger, I mean. Maybe that part is true," Ann says.

"That's right," Penny agrees, nodding her head.

"It could be," I say, weighing the possibility.

Ann puts a steady hand on my shoulder. "Do you think he knows?"

"I'm thinking it more and more," I say, feeling a spasm stretch across my stomach. "He was over this morning and it sounds like he has a lot riding on these houses going up. Hopefully Ms. Barry can help today. Did you guys try the door yet?"

"We were waiting for you," Penny answers.

We cross the road and bang on her door, but nobody answers. We circle around to the back to see if there's another door. But the back door is locked too and there's no answer. However, we do spy the book about tea-leaf readings on her kitchen table, the one we wanted to take out a few months ago. It's got colourful sticky notes jabbing out from its pages. It's clear Ms. Barry is totally into this book. No wonder it was never available at the library. Maybe she has more in common with the pack than we thought? Ms. Barry is nowhere to be found.

"Seriously. What are we going to do? What if Roger kidnapped—"

"Penny! This is no time for dramatics. Keep it together," Ann says. "Maybe she stayed overnight as an extra precaution to safeguard her bees. Let's not jump to conclusions, yet."

"But—"

"Penny, don't freak out. I'm sure she's fine. We'll find her," Brandi says in a comforting tone.

"Next steps, you guys? What do we do now?" Ann asks.

"Okay, let me think. My mom said they have a meeting with the city this morning, so everything is still moving forward. I know we were hoping Ms. Barry could help us, and we don't have the photos, but we do have the pictures Ann and I drew. I think we should go to the police and tell them what we know. We can hand over the drawings as evidence and they could go and see the pictographs for themselves. We can also tell them about how Ms. Barry was supposed to meet us and help us and that she might possibly be missing," I say, talking super fast.

"I think you're right. It's time we come clean," Ann says with complete confidence. "Besides, even Ms. Barry would have contacted the authorities by now."

"Exactly." A chill spreads over me, freezing me from the inside like an ice cream headache. "Okay, let's do this." I stare down the open road. "Are you in?" I ask them, hoping for a yes.

"I'm in," they say.

Even Penny.

CHAPTER 33

It takes us almost thirty minutes on our bikes down the sidewalks and through the trails to arrive at the downtown police station. The building looks like a rectangular grey cement block. I've never been inside it before. It doesn't seem inviting, except for the large maple tree extending its branches and the colourful flags flapping in the wind. There are also irises and rudbeckias planted in front. I'm getting super good at identifying flowers.

I thrust open the heavy glass door and see several people in uniform zigzagging across the hall, holding clipboards and coffees. Everyone looks like they're on their way somewhere. I stop an officer who's gripping a steaming mug of coffee in each hand.

"Excuse me, I have some information to share."

"Is that so?" She bends down. "What about?"

"Well." I suck in a large and bottomless breath. "We found some pictographs inside the mountain, and it's really—"

"Leclair!" A man in plain clothes bellows from behind her. "I've got this."

"You sure, Detective? They just came off the street. I can take their statement."

"Nah, you head into the morning meeting. It looks like your hands are full already."

I glance at Ann and she raises her shoulders.

"Young ladies, let's talk in here." The man motions us to a large room with a wooden table and eight chairs. "My name is Detective Belinski. Do your parents know you're here?"

Detective Belinski has shiny grey hair and yellowish teeth. He also has bushy, greying eyebrows and a large, square chin. He's not wearing a uniform. His pants are grey and his shirt is long-sleeved and blue. He must be the undercover kind of police officer.

"No," I tell him, feeling the guilt surface for not telling my mom yet.

He takes out his small black notebook and jots down some notes. He smiles at us, which makes his eyes squint. "Okay, what are your names?" he asks. "First and last, please."

"Do we have to?" Penny asks, her voice trembling.

"Well, it's standard procedure when you give a statement like this. You're not in any trouble."

So we give him our names and addresses and then we tell him all about the Northwood Heights development, about Roger and Carling King Construction, about removing the orange flags and bands, about the pictographs and the mountain that will soon be destroyed and about how Ms. Barry is hypothetically missing. I really hope we won't be in trouble for removing those flags. There's no taking it back now. My eyes blink fast but my heart raps faster, waiting for his response.

"This is quite a story you've shared here." He points to the pad with his ballpoint pen.

"It's not a story. It's the truth." Brandi stands up.

"I'm not saying I don't believe you. You seem like nice girls, smart girls—"

"We are. We're very smart," Ann says.

"The smartest," Penny adds.

"Of course. I'm just saying, these are serious allegations you've made."

"Well, can you help us?" I ask him. "Will you go and check it out today, because waiting any longer could—"

"Listen, I can assure you that I will personally see to this. That's a promise." He gestures with his hands to add emphasis.

"And Ms. Barry?" Penny says, her eyes moon-wide with worry. Is she wearing mascara?

"I'll look into that, too," he assures us. "Anything else?" he asks before closing the tiny notepad in his hands.

"The drawings," Ann replies. We take our notebooks from

our backpacks and hand them to the detective. "We drew the pictographs," she tells him.

"Is that so?" he says.

"We really want to save this cultural artifact," I say in a non-negotiable tone.

"Of course. Of course." He nods. "Listen, it's probably best that you don't tell your parents or anyone else about this until I look into it. I wouldn't want to tip off Roger or anyone on his payroll. Is that clear?"

"We won't say a word," Penny tells him, but I'm quiet.

"What will you do after you see them?" Ann asks.

"Here. Take my card. Call me later this evening. I should have some information for you by seven tonight."

"Thank you, Detective Belinski," I say.

"Thank you for coming in, ladies. You did the right thing." He slants his head forward and shuts the door.

"Well, that went well," Brandi says, unlocking her bike.

"I guess so." I look back at the door.

"What do you mean, you guess so?"

"I don't know," I answer as the leaves on the maple tree shake with a gust of wind, like they're trying to get my attention. "Why would he ask us not to tell our parents? That doesn't seem right."

"Huh, that's a good point." Brandi sighs. "But, you heard him, he said he doesn't want to risk the news getting out."

Penny hops on her bike.

"I heard what he said," I answer back. My stomach churns.

"I think Wolf is right," Ann replies. "He didn't seem *that* concerned."

"Ann, hold on to that card he gave you. We may need to call him later, or show our parents, if we need to," I tell her.

"I won't let it out of my sight," she says. "So, what now? Do you want to hang out for a bit?" Ann asks. "It's the weekend, after all."

"Sorry, I'm going to visit the Big Nickel with my cousins visiting from Timmins." Brandi shrugs. "It seems that's *all* tourists want to do when they come here—get a photo taken with the largest nickel in the world."

"It is our claim to fame," I say.

"I can't hang out either. I have family stuff," Penny says.

"Shoot, me either. I told my mom I'd stop by Grandma Houle's. She asked me to check in on her now that she's out of the hospital."

"Okay, then," Ann says, slightly miffed. "What happened to spending more time together?"

"There's still later this afternoon," Penny answers. I notice her hair is different, in a French braid.

"Fine. Later," Ann replies, before riding off.

We scatter away on our bikes, each with a different place to go. I was hoping to feel a hundred percent better after telling the police everything, but I don't exactly feel reassured and I'm not sure why.

So much is at risk of being lost. And even with Brandi and Penny on friendly terms, the pack still feels like it's unravelling.

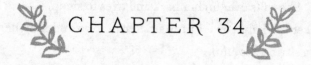

CHAPTER 34

Grandma doesn't open the door, even after I knock our secret knock of three fast, then two slow, plus two fast. I try the handle. It's open, so I step inside.

"Grandma? Grandma? It's me, Wolf. Are you here?"

The house is eerily quiet and she's not sitting on her favourite flowery upholstered chair in the living room, the one she's coined the lazy-girl, or at the kitchen table with the tiny TV on. She's not on the back porch either. I continue to her bedroom and find her lying in bed, with a glass of water and half a dozen jars of pills by her bedside. There's also an old photo album sprawled open beside her, with black-and-white photos glued inside.

"Grandma." I nudge her gently.

"Wolf, it's you," she says with a thin smile, making her soft wrinkles spread across her cheeks. "I thought I was dreaming again. These pills sure make an old lady question her marbles." She rolls over on her back and tries to sit up.

"Let me help you." I prop up her pillows and help her get into a sitting position.

"Thank you, dear." She pats the bed and I get in beside her, but only on top of the covers.

"What are all these, Grandma?" I point to the album, trying not to look at all the pills again.

"I was just looking at old photos of my parents, when we used to live near Golden Lake." She pulls the photo album across her lap and points to a photo. "This one here is my favourite memory: Summer Solstice with all of my aunts, uncles and cousins. We got together every year, no matter what, to celebrate the longest day of the year. It was a big celebration where we gave thanks for the sun and for the land, for the water and all of the animals too. That's why I used to make such a big fuss with you all on the first day of summer. Well, at least when you were younger. These days everyone is so busy and living in different cities . . ." Her voice trails off.

"I remember the fires we used to have in your backyard and the decorations you would hang from the trees. All the glowing lanterns. It was so pretty, Grandma. We should bring it back next year."

"You're right. Let's make sure we plan an extra-special one.

We'll send invitations out and everything. And we'll stay up until the sun rises."

I nestle into her.

She points to another photo. "I remember this one of my daddy and me was taken right after we came back from fishing. Those were the days, Wolf. There were so many fish back then, they would nearly jump in our boat. Now, we have sit for hours for a little nibble on the line, and too often, the fish are just too small to keep."

"Your daddy was tall," I say.

"He sure was. Like you. I actually see so much of him in you. You have my father's spirit."

"I do?" I feel a sunrise in my heart. I keep looking at the photos. "Wow, he had long hair," I say.

"He always did. It was so shiny and strong. The envy of all the women in our family."

I bring the album closer to my face. "He has your eyes, Grandma. They look kind."

She smiles. "It's important to remember our loved ones, dear. Even after they are long gone. You know, I believe they're always with us. My parents are still in my heart." Grandma grabs my hand. "Just like both Poppy and me will always be close, in your heart."

"But you're here, you're here with me right now."

"Oh, Wolf." She brings my hand to her heart. "I am and I always will be. Whether or not I'm here inside this house, or in the trampoline Olympics, upstairs." She points to the ceiling. "I'll always be by your side, just in a different way." She kisses the top of my head.

"I never want to think about you being gone." My eyes fill with water.

"We have to. It's the hard truth. I won't be here forever, love."

I tuck my head under her arm and let my tears stain her blue cotton nightdress.

Grandma strokes my back and lets me cry. "You can never lose who you truly love. Remember that." She leans her head against mine. "I really do adore your snazzy hair," she says. "Maybe I should get a matching hairdo."

I smile through my tears at the thought.

We listen to the chickadees outside the window, calling to each other.

"You're the best granddaughter a grandma could ever ask for."

"I'm not perfect, Grandma, remember? I'm sorry I wasn't here when you needed me."

"Oh that. Forget about that night. Nobody's perfect, sweet pea. I sure ain't."

"Well you're a perfect grandma, that's for sure."

"Thank you, but that's probably because I was, and still am, such a flawed mother."

"Grandma!"

"It's true. Why do you think your auntie and your uncle have stayed away for so long? I drive them bonkers. And your mom, well, we're not exactly in the get-along gang."

"Mom is really hard to talk to. She's like that with me too. Sometimes I wish she was more like you."

"Your mom does her best. She's a hard worker and she loves you very much."

"It just feels like she's so different than us. I don't get it. Why doesn't she like nature? How can you not like trees? And why doesn't she believe in the stories you share with me, in the traditions?"

"It's complicated."

"That's what she said."

"Well, it's true. It was harder when she was growing up. Not many people around here wanted to hear about tree talkers, for one thing."

"But why? I think it's one of the best things about our family."

"I'm really glad to hear you say that. But it was harder for your mom, back then. It wasn't always easy for her at school. Kids can be real cruel. Adults too. Even some of her teachers gave her a hard time. She did what she had to do to survive. Which for her meant leaving behind some of the traditions."

"But what about now? Couldn't she bring them back now?"

"Maybe. You never know." She smiles a sad smile that reminds me of the months after Poppy died when she was trying to wear a smile to disguise her sadness. I can tell the difference.

"Grandma, remember when you told me about the pictographs? When your daddy showed you, in the canoe?"

"Oh yes!" Her face lights up like a bright star. "I do. They were the prettiest pictures."

"Can you describe them? What they looked like?"

"Well, the ones I remember the most showed hunters catching their prey. And there was one of the Great Lynx, which my father told me was the spirit of the water. He spoke often about them and the ones he saw as a boy, over in the Ottawa Valley. The drawings are filled with prophecies and stories, medicines and songs."

"What kinds of stories do they tell, exactly?"

"All kinds. Daddy told me they were mostly night stories, about dreams and visions. It was a way for our ancestors to record their thoughts and their feelings, like a dream journal. Some of them were also predictions, like an ancient farmer's almanac, or prayers for good health and good hunting."

I snuggle in closer.

"Why so much interest in pictographs anyway?" she asks sleepily. She puts the album to the side and pulls up her covers.

I think about telling her right now. I think about telling her absolutely everything, about Roger and Ms. Barry, but I glance at the many jars of pills by her bedside and I can see that her eyes have grown heavy again.

"Oh, it's nothing, really. I just remember you sharing these memories with me when we went camping in River Valley that time, and I wanted to remember it more clearly."

"Well, all right, then. I'm glad you asked," she says, her eyes almost closed.

I sit up and tuck my grandma in. "I think that's it for today." I kiss her crinkled cheek.

"All right, dear. How about tomorrow I teach you how to make my famous sweet bannock? Prepare to be utterly amazed," she murmurs with her eyes now completely closed. I wipe my tear-stained face with the bottom of my T-shirt and close her bedroom door.

CHAPTER 35

I hate seeing Grandma weakening and in pain. So much so, I'm pedalling hard to push the ache away from inside my chest. My legs burn as I climb up the large hill towards my house. I pass the school, now closed for the summer, and right before I'm out of range, I swear I spot Roger's truck driving towards the back. Why would he drive to the back of the school?

I know it's probably not a good idea, because I feel warning prickles on my skin, but I decide to follow him. I turn into the parking lot and head back the opposite way. I get off my bike and walk it slowly, past the monkey bars and the see-saw, until I hear two car doors slamming shut. I peer around the corner but there's a row of thick cedars blocking my view. I squint in the sun, and I see a man I recognize take a step past the tree line. It's Detective Belinski, the officer we spoke to this morning. Bushy grey eyebrows and square jaw. What is he doing here? He's talking to someone. Is it Roger? I can't tell. The other person is completely hidden from view, but the detective's hands are moving in frantic circles and he looks very upset. He paces back and forth in the gravel and then stomps his feet. Then I hear his truck pull away and drive off, spitting rocks as he leaves. I tuck myself behind overgrown shrubs, completely out of sight. When I look again, Roger's company truck is racing around the bend, leaving a giant cloud of dust behind. Even after he's gone, my heart still clatters like a jackhammer.

Detective Belinski is definitely not happy. Who was he talking to? Was it Roger? He must have seen the pictographs. I need to talk to one of the girls. I decide to go see Ann, who lives just around the corner from the school.

I pull up to her house and I don't even bother with the kickstand. I drop my bike on the grass, race up to the front door and knock frantically.

"Oh! Mrs. McFadden, you're home."

"I am. What is it dear? You look upset." Her forehead crumples and her eyes stare into mine like she's trying to read my mind.

"Oh. No, of course not," I strain to steady my voice.

"Well, come on in. I'll go find Ann," she says. I follow her and wait at the bottom of the stairs.

"Wolf? What is it?" Ann looks concerned as she slides her hand down the banister and skids down the stairs in her bare feet.

"More developments. Big developments."

"Let's go up to my room."

We charge up the stairs, and she closes the door to her bedroom and locks it. Her walls are covered with photos of Egyptian pyramids and pharaohs. Planets and stars dangle from her ceiling, twirling in circles above us. "What happened? Didn't you go see your grandma?"

I sit on the floor and lean against her bed. Ann sits across from me on the thick carpet. My heart throbs at the mere mention of Grandma's name. "Yeah, I was there. But when I was on my way back home, I saw his truck."

"Whose truck?"

"Roger's company truck."

"Where?"

"Well, actually, I don't know if it was Roger. I never actually saw him, exactly." I rake my hands through my hair. "But it was definitely his company truck."

"Isn't there more than one?"

"Yes," I say. "Anyway, I saw the truck pull into the school. I thought it was odd, so I followed him."

"Oh, no. That was risky."

"I know. But it's a good thing I did because I saw them. Well, kind of."

"Them? Who's them? Your mom and—"

"No! Detective Belinski and somebody else who might or might not be Roger!"

"What?" Ann finally looks like she's getting it.

"Yes! They were talking behind the school and Detective Belinski did not look happy. Like on a scale of how angry he looked, from one to ten, he was at a twenty—off the charts!"

"Did you hear what they said?"

"No. I couldn't get close enough. I was afraid they would see me."

"Of course."

"But no matter what was said, it's pretty obvious that he's furious with Roger or someone working for Roger." I dig my head into my palm.

"But that's good, right? Isn't that what we want? Do you think he already checked out the pictographs?"

"I assume so."

"But . . ." Ann pauses and I can see her brain working something out. "Why would he talk to Roger or not-Roger behind the school and not talk to him at the site or take him into the police station for questioning?"

"I don't know." I rub my forehead. "I knew something felt off about it. Why be so secretive?"

Ann's eyebrows arch like triangles. A long pause. "Do you think the detective already knew?"

"What? No." But the thought nags at me. "That would be really, really bad," I say.

"The worst."

I start crying. I can't help it. All of it just comes crashing onto me. Ann puts her hand on my shoulder. I try to clear my throat but then Esmeralda pops into my head. Her flaming fingernails. Her warnings. How this summer was going to be the biggest test, how everything would change. My heart hurts.

Ann pulls on my arm, gently. "What does this mean for Ms. Barry?" She gets up and sits on the edge of her bed.

"I'm not sure."

"You know what?" she says. "Let's just get to the bottom of this right now. Let's call Detective Belinski. We'll use my sister's phone. She's at softball practice."

We don't even turn on the lights in her sister's room, just in case someone walks by in the hallway.

"Do you want me to do the talking?" Ann asks.

I pick up the phone. "That's okay, I can handle this."

Ann passes me his business card and my fear slithers out. I exhale and dial the numbers carefully.

"Hello, Mr.—I mean Detective Belinksi, please."

Ann gives me a nod.

I tilt the phone so she can hear.

"What is this concerning, miss?"

"My name is Wolf Lagacé, and I'm calling to get an update on what my friends and I discussed earlier today."

"I'm sorry, but he's left for the day and he may not be back for a few days. Do you want to leave a message?"

"Is there another way to reach him?"

"I'm afraid not."

"Never mind. Thank you." I hang up the phone.

"I feel like we're moving in circles," I say. "First Ms. Barry is missing and now Detective Belinski is away and not available. It's time we come clean to our parents."

"I agree. Before anyone else goes missing."

Truth bumps spread across my arms.

"What if they don't believe us?" Ann says. "Detective Belinski has our drawings now."

"I know. And what if Roger destroys the proof before we can convince them to go see it for themselves?"

"Let's call Penny and see if her dad is back with his camera. We were going to meet up after dinner. Let's get some photos before we tell them everything." Ann crosses her arms.

"Can you call the girls to let them know? I'll meet you at Birchwood."

"No problem," she says.

My heart thuds all the way up to my throat. "Ann, what if my mom *does* know about the pictographs?"

She curls in her lips and takes my hand. "Let's deal with one thing at a time," she says.

CHAPTER 36

M s. Barry is still AWOL. No signs of her anywhere. I backtracked to her place after a quick, necessary wardrobe change at home before hightailing it to Birchwood. According to the law, she could officially be declared a missing person since it's been over twenty-four hours since we last saw her. I feel super guilty to have involved her like this.

The sun is starting to set and we're meeting under the five birch trees. If only they could help us. I ask them to, first without words, because even if there is the smallest chance, I'm going to try. And then, I go ahead and whisper out loud, "Please watch over us tonight."

Once the girls arrive, we all cram inside the cabin, sitting in a circle with our knees touching. Every single one of us is wearing black so we're not easy to see on the property.

"We've had some fun times in here." Brandi flips her hood off.

"The best," Ann says. "No matter what happens, they can't take that away from us."

"That's true," I say, "but let's not give up before it's over. Is everyone ready for this?" I ask.

"I brought the camera and some extra film," Penny says. "There's already one roll in the camera but I'm not sure how many photos are left on it."

My belly flip-flops with anxiety. "This is our last mission to help save Birchwood."

"No biggie." Brandi gives an awkward smile.

"Forevermore," I say.

"All in," Brandi says.

"For Ms. Barry," Ann says.

"For the pictographs!" Penny declares.

Before we head up the mountain, we narrate our pledge. It feels super important tonight. While I hold Brandi and Ann's hands, I look at my friends and the Birch Family standing on guard around us. I feel them in my heart. I feel them cheering us on. It's almost as if they are leaning in around us too.

One, two, three, four,
Together today and forevermore.
Friendship first, always true,
Northern Star lead us through.

"Let's do this!" Brandi flips her hood back over her head.

I crack a smile and file into line. This is a major undercover operation. Our last chance to get proof. We leave our bikes buried in the bushes. It's harder to hide on a bike with the reflectors. We begin our trek up the black mountain, following the winding path. There's a cool breeze tonight that helps to keep the mosquitoes away and the crescent moon is barely visible through the night clouds, which all works to our advantage.

Once we reach the NO TRESPASSING sign, Ann squeals, "I see lights!"

"We should have expected someone would be guarding the premises," I whisper.

Penny puts a hand on my back.

"Let's keep silent as we make our way up," Ann mutters.

I sidle to the front. "Stay close to each other," I tell them, lowering the hood over my head.

As if on cue, an owl hoots and I feel Penny grip my shirt and pull me back. I suck in my breath and we keep pressing forward, slowly, listening for any footsteps or voices ahead. The smell of wildflowers whips around me. All of my senses are on high alert. As we approach the clearing and the hacked stumps, a radio walkie-talkie screeches and cuts the silence.

"Ten-four, Mr. Biggs, where you at? Over."

"I'm at the site, St. Patrick, all clear. Over."

"We've got a situation at Zone Six. We need muscle. Over."

"I'm not supposed to leave under any circumstances. We're prepping for tomorrow's blast. Over. The dynamite has been delivered. Over."

"This is a level-three situation. It'll take less than ten minutes. Remember, you owe me one. Over."

"Don't remind me." The man moans. "This makes us even. I'll be there in five. Over."

For once, I think, something is going our way. We wait until this guy, Mr. Biggs, hikes into his truck, and we exhale a huge sigh of relief as he drives down the man-made gravel lane.

"We need to act fast."

We disperse. Ann and I move quickly, scurrying up the mountain, our adrenaline helping us climb to the large boulder.

"Ann, you'll have to hold the flashlight while I take the photos."

"Hurry!" she says. "And use the flash!" Ann is frantic, her ponytail swinging madly. "It's so dark, Wolf. What if it doesn't show up on film?"

"We have to try. This is our LAST chance." I snap about three photos and the film ends.

"Hand me the other roll," I tell her. I snap it in quickly and crank it forward.

"Girls! Hurry!" Brandi says from below.

I snap several other photos, but I'm not keeping count. I'm just trying to focus on taking the best shot. I don't want to miss any. We hear wheels crunch against the gravel road. Ann and I scoot down the mountain like pro mountaineers. I hand the camera and film off to Penny, and we dart back into the woods to hide behind the bushes until the headlights click off. Then we tiptoe all the way down the path, as quickly as possible. That is, until Brandi runs smack into a body—Detective Belinski.

"Well, well, well. Didn't I tell you ladies to stay away from this place?" He's wearing a ball cap. I can barely see his eyes.

"And what are you doing here, Detective?" Ann's standing on her toes. "Aren't you supposed to be away?" I notice that she's nearly as tall as him.

"Just checking on things. Like I told you I would. You should get home now. Before I call your parents."

"Maybe you should," Penny says.

"What's that you're holding, dear? Is that a—"

Penny passes the camera to Ann and Ann to me. I slip the camera in the front pocket of my sweatshirt.

"It's a flashlight," I snap back.

"Don't let this grey hair fool you. My eyes are not as old as you think."

"We need to get home," Penny says. "I wouldn't want my dad coming out to look for me."

"Right. Straight home, now," he says. "But first, I'll take this." He lunges towards me and seizes the camera from my pocket.

"You can't take that!" I yell, stepping in closer.

"Actually, you're all trespassing, so I wouldn't argue," he says sternly. He pops the camera open and rips out the film. "Is this all of it?" he asks.

Penny drops the other roll in his hands. "Here," she says.

What did Penny just do?

"Thanks." He smiles a toothy smile. "I'll need this for my report. Hurry on, now."

We all take off running down the hill as fast as we can until we reach our bikes behind the cedars.

We collapse onto the ground, gasping.

"Now what?" Brandi says. "There goes everything."

"Not if he's on our side. He said it was for his report," Penny says.

Ann turns onto her stomach and props herself onto her elbows. "But what if he's not on our side? Then what?"

"Then we have no proof," I say, feeling completely discouraged and disheartened.

Penny sits up. She pulls out a roll of film from her pocket and holds it up to the dark night sky.

"No way!" Brandi says.

"But how?" I ask her.

She grins. "I gave him an empty container."

"There's still hope," Brandi says.

Penny cradles the film carefully in both hands.

"Tonight we tell our parents everything," I say. "This has gotten way out of hand, and Ms. Barry is still missing."

"Majorly," Penny says. "But, Wolf, you take the film. I'd never forgive myself if I lost it."

"Okay, I will. Great job, Penny!" I carefully tuck the film inside my front pocket. "Let's hope we have something to show from this."

"Yeah," Ann says. "How about we regroup tomorrow and fill each other in on everything."

"If we're not all grounded for life. It's definitely going to be a long night of explaining," Brandi says, like she's dreading it more than anything.

Understatement of the century.

CHAPTER 37

I don't want to rush home. How can I tell Mom what's been going on? What if she already knows? There's no winning here. Either she gets her heart broken or I do, by finding out that Mom has known the truth all along.

The sky is still the colour of black ink. Not a single star is shining. Thoughts of Grandma swirl in my head. I think about one day not being able to visit or talk with her. There are so many knots and tangles in my heart. I just keep pedalling hard and fast, and all of a sudden I find myself circling in front of Hari's house. I must be losing my marbles, too, because now I'm in his backyard, on my tippytoes tapping on his bedroom window.

Hari rubs his eyes with his fists. His hair is sticking up. "What are you doing here? You okay?"

"I uh, um. Well. No. Not really." I'm fighting back the monsoon inside me.

"What's wrong?"

I bite the inside of my cheeks. "Everything."

"I'm coming out," he says.

I watch Hari climb out of his window and jump five feet to the ground. He's wearing a Star Wars T-shirt and track pants. He's also wearing the bracelet I gave him with the yellow bead.

He ambles over to me and I don't know what to say. I count the daisies lining the side of the house. It helps to calm me. "How are you? How have you been, I mean."

"Things are still really hard, even more so since the funeral and now that everyone has left." He pauses for a moment, but then keeps going. "Mom is really sad. She barely gets out of bed now, and my brother is gone most the time with his friends. To be honest, it's too quiet around here."

"I'm so sorry. I wish I could do something."

"I know," he says. I can feel warmth coming off his skin. "Let's go over there"—he points—"by the tree."

I push my bike across the yard and he walks barefoot beside me. The crickets are louder than ever. I lean against the willow tree, with its arms drooping over us, and hear the branches sway. "Hari, are you going to be okay? Like really okay?"

"Eventually, I guess. I don't think I'll ever not miss him though, you know?"

"Of course." The tears spill down my cheeks.

"Wolf?" He grabs my arms and squeezes gently.

"It's my grandma." My lips tremble. "She's sick, and she's—" I hang my head. I can't believe I'm letting him see me like this.

"I'm sorry," he says in the softest voice. "I know how close you are." And then, he leans into me, awkwardly, and puts both of his arms around me, like a hug.

"They say it gets better," he whispers in my ear. "Bit by bit, a tiny fraction at a time, even if I don't quite believe it yet. But that's what people have been telling me."

I can feel his heart beating against mine.

"Hari," I say, and look up at him with my tear-sodden face. "I'm sorry we haven't talked since school ended. I haven't been a great friend. I've been sucking at pretty much everything these days."

"Wolf, we're not friends."

"We're not?" I answer, confusion filling my cloudy brain.

"We're actually more than friends." He stares into my eyes. My heart seriously thumps like crazy, like the Bugs Bunny cartoon characters I used to watch. Then, under the gloomy and dark sky, without a single sparkling star as far as the eye can see, he leans in to kiss me. Our noses bump and then he finds my lips and I find his, and we kiss. My head is spinning. My heart is thudding.

I feel like I just stepped off a merry-go-round.

After the kiss, we sit down under the tree and lean our backs against the trunk. My heart is still dancing in my chest and I'm breathing in the cool night air and staring up again into the empty sky. I think back to just a few months ago, when our pack's biggest problem was trying to find something fun to do on a Saturday night like read tea leaves. Things were so simple then.

Why does thirteen have to be one emotional, awkward and confusing moment after another? Even the good ones?

"Lost in space there, Lagacé?"

"Ha. Kind of." I grin with total embarrassment. "Speaking of space, Hari Patel, do you think UFOs really exist?" I try to change the subject.

"I'm not sure." He stares up into the night. "You?"

"I want to believe. I don't know," I answer, feeling awkward once again. "What about, do you, um, do you believe in heaven?" I immediately regret asking the question in case it hurts his feelings to even think about it. I pinch the inside of my wrist nervously and wait for his answer.

"I really hope there's a heaven." He grabs my hand, gently.

"Me too." I stretch my legs out in front of me.

I want to lighten things up a little, and so I continue blurting stuff out. "I found out my great-granddaddy was a tree talker. He was able to communicate *with* trees."

He turns his head and looks me in the eye. "Seriously?"

"Yeah. I've started trying to talk to them as well," I say proudly, like I'm ready for people to know.

"You are the strangest and most interesting girl I know."

I smile the brightest smile.

A fire truck screams in the distance and everything comes colliding back, especially the part where I have to tell my mom tonight. Despite wanting to stay here forever, holding his hand under the dim sky, I manage to pull myself up from the cool grass, from Hari.

"I should get going."

"Let me walk you home." He springs to his feet.

"I have my bike," I say, walking towards it now.

"Still, I should."

"You should go back to sleep, Hari Patel. Plus, you're in your pyjamas." I point.

"That doesn't matter, and if I sleep now, I'll wake up thinking it never happened."

"I'll remind you." I stare into his kind and sad and dreamy eyes.

"Wolf."

"Yes?"

"I'm glad you came by."

"You are."

"Yeah."

Suddenly, the leaves on the trees start shivering in the wind, echoing the stirring inside my stomach. I manage to get on my bike and weave away from him standing under the willow. I look back and he's still there, gazing at me in his Star Wars T-shirt and bare feet. He's smiling. And so am I.

I can feel my face stretching as I ride away, knowing why all the night stars aren't hanging above in the sky—because they're all blazing inside of me. Every last one.

How can the best things and the worst things happen on the exact same day?

CHAPTER 38

I park my bike in the shed and walk past the door to make a beeline to my bedroom window when the outside light flicks on and washes me in a silver light. I freeze. I don't move a muscle. I turn into cold stone.

"Wolf! Get in here. Now!"

I scurry into the house and let Mom do the talking. She's wearing her pink housecoat with her furry, black slippers. She tightens the belt around her waist and locks the door behind me.

"Mom—"

"Not a single word. I don't know who you think you are coming home so late. I thought you learned your lesson when Grandma— And now, I have too much to worry about, without having to be alarmed about my thirteen-year-old out at this hour."

"But Mom—"

"I've had a really long day and I'm tired and I don't want to do this right now. We are going to talk about this first thing in the morning. Then, you will tell me everything." She gets up to walk away.

I swallow hard. "I don't think it can wait. It's about Roger."

She spins around. "What about Roger?"

Guilt hitches itself to my stomach like a suction cup. It's true, she already looks tired. She has dark half moons under her eyes that remind me of Grandma. I don't want to add to her list of worries, but I know I have to tell her.

"What is it, Wolf?" She asks again and sits down at the kitchen table. She cups her hands together.

I count to three Mississippis. I've been holding everything in for so long and I want to tell her absolutely everything.

"I, um, I don't know how to say this."

"You're scaring me. Tell me now."

"Okay, here goes. My friends and I, we found pictographs—real, ancient pictographs hidden inside the mountain."

"Pictographs? What are you talking about? What mountain?"

I try to slow my speech, but my heart is racing. "The mountaintop that's being developed into Northwood Heights. I think Roger knows about them and he's still planning to destroy it. We found one of his tape measures—"

"That's not possible. It can't be." She clutches the table.

"It's true. You have to believe me. They could be like a thousand years old or more!"

An army of dark creases marks her forehead. She rakes her fingers through her hair, and that's when I see something catch the light. A shimmering sparkle on her finger. I look again and spot a diamond ring. This is not happening. No, no, no, no.

"Are you engaged?" I ask. The question fires out of my mouth like lightning.

Mom looks down at her hand, like she's surprised to see it, like she forgot the ring was even there. She covers it with her other hand. "I was going to tell you. It just happened, tonight."

I stand up. "You can't marry him."

Mom tucks her hair behind her ears. She weaves her hands together on the table. "Listen. I speak to Roger every day and he never mentioned this. He cares about this town. We both do. Sweetheart, I know you don't agree with his business, but seriously, this is too much. To make something up like this? You're going to have to accept him. We're getting married."

"Please! You have to believe me." Both of my hands are clenched into fists. "I'm not making this up. We went to the police station and everything!"

"You went where?" She gets up and sits right back down at the table, her elbows against the wood, and both hands in her hair.

"Mom, there's more. Ms. Barry is missing. Ever since we asked her to help us. She was supposed to meet us at the mountain and now we can't find her." I finally burst into tears.

Mom is shaking her head from side to side, pushing her fingers deep into her hairline.

"This makes absolutely no sense. I've been up there and I never saw a thing. Roger has never mentioned any problems. He never mentioned anything about pictographs. And why would you go to the librarian and the police, and not tell *me* first? You should have come to me."

"Why would I? You don't even believe me." I stare at her ring. "He's not who you think he is."

"You're a kid, I know you think you're all grown up but there are some things you just don't understand yet. He wanted to be here tonight, for us to tell you together. But I said I needed to tell you first. He cares about you. He wants to us be a family."

"Really? What is *so* good about him anyways? Seriously!"

"So many things! He's a hard worker, for one thing, and he employs lots of people in this town. They have jobs because of him. He sees the potential in everything. He wants to make things beautiful."

"Concrete doesn't make things pretty, Mom."

"Don't you think I can make good decisions for us?"

I'm so upset, my mouth continues to spray more words. "You can't marry him, and if you do, I'll go live with Grandma."

"That's enough. I don't want to hear another word."

I tear away from the kitchen table, lock my bedroom door, fall into bed and curl up into a small ball. Once the anger settles, I actually start to feel sad for Mom because I realize that the best thing and the worst thing happened to her on the same day too.

CHAPTER 39

I wake up to the sound of tapping. I roll over and the tap becomes more like a knock. It sounds like someone is at the front door. I throw on my housecoat and rattle down the stairs and peek through the peephole. I see a tall man wearing a red shirt with blue shorts. He looks like a messenger. He's holding an envelope in his hands. I slowly open the door, keeping the chain on the hook.

"Good morning, miss. I apologize for waking you this morning. This message was marked urgent. It must be for your mom, a Wolf Lagacé?"

"Oh," I answer, covering up my yawn.

"Please make sure she gets it." He slides it through the small opening of the door. By the time I look up again, he's zipped down the end of the street on his bicycle, almost like he was never here.

I close the door and examine the white envelope. There's no return address. Just my name and home address printed across it, with the word URGENT in red. I sit at the kitchen table and open it.

Dear Wolf,

My sincere apologies for not showing up as promised to help you with your quandary. I was indisposed, you see, because Farmer Johnson was kindly helping me with my bees when he was stung. Unbeknownst to him, he had a severe allergy and required immediate medical attention. I've been helping with the neces-sary and numerous farm chores. Please know that I will be back soon and will finally be able to assist you as promised.

Sincerely,
Ms. B

The phone rings, jolting me. I'm still trying to decide if I'm dreaming or if I'm really awake.

"Wolf, it's Ann."

"Ann, am I awake?" I ask.

"What are you talking about?" she says. "Hang on, I need to change phones, my parents are at it again."

I wait until I hear her click the phone and pick up the other one.

"What's going on?" I stare at the letter in my hands.

"The usual. They argue about everything these days. You name it. The latest argument, though, was about me. They caught me sneaking in last night."

"Oh no! You too."

"Wait. Your mom caught you?"

"Yeah. I guess it was bound to happen eventually."

"Yup. Law of averages."

"So, did you tell them about everything, then?"

"No." Ann sighs. "Dad had to leave for his night shift and Mom just sent me to my room and I've been hiding out since then. I plan to try again once my dad gets back this morning."

"Sorry, Ann."

"What about you?"

"It was World War III here last night."

"Seriously?"

"It was horrible. She doesn't believe me. She thinks Roger's the best man that has ever lived. And the worst part is, they got engaged yesterday."

"What? That boggles my mind! I'm so sorry. What the heck do we do now?"

"We need to get that film developed. I didn't think I was really going to need to prove the pictographs exist, but it looks like I do."

"We're running out of options and people to help us," Ann says.

"Actually, you won't believe this, but I received a message from Ms. Barry this morning."

"A message? What kind of message?"

"A letter delivered by a messenger on a bike."

"What did it say?"

"She said that her bees stung Farmer Johnson when he was helping her and he had an allergic reaction."

"Well, that's why we couldn't find her."

"Mystery solved."

"At least now we know she wasn't kidnapped."

"Exactly."

"Let's get those photos developed." I check my Swatch. "Meet me at the corner of Vine and Gemmell in twenty minutes?"

"I'll be there."

"Thanks."

"And, Wolf, I'm really sorry about your mom's engagement."

"Thanks," I say, feeling the lump in my throat again. "I'm sorry about your parents fighting so much. That sounds really hard."

"Yeah, it is," she says with a small voice before hanging up.

Besides the news about Ms. Barry, I still sense a dozen thunderclouds swelling in my belly. It feels like a hundred percent chance of precipitation. Guaranteed.

CHAPTER 40

The summer sky is super blue this morning, nothing like last night. It's cloudless and clear. We park our bikes and lock them up outside of Black's Photography. The bell jingles as we enter the small storefront.

"She looks familiar," Ann whispers.

"Didn't she work at our school?"

"Hello there! You two go to Rockwood Public School, right? I used to work in the cafeteria."

"That's right! I remember." I nod.

"Off to high school next year?"

Ann says, "That's us! Nice to see you again, Mrs.—"

"Bisaillon. But please, call me Iris. So what can I help you with today?"

"Oh yeah," I say. "I know it usually takes a day or two to process a roll of film, but if it's not too much trouble, would it be possible to get it done now?"

"Kids want everything yesterday, don't they?" She snorts. "Well, girls, you're in luck because I just finished processing all of the other jobs and you are my first customers of the day. Let's get this roll printed, trimmed and tucked inside that envelope in a jiffy."

"Great! Thank you so much Mrs.—I mean, Iris. Thank you," Ann says.

"I'm happy to make someone's day. Why don't you go and get yourselves a couple of drinks, and by the time you come back, it should be ready to go."

"Good idea," I say.

We head straight inside Ted's Confectionary. We both decide on a cold orange drink, since it's still morning and all. After we pay, we go back outside to sit at the picnic table under a large green umbrella to shade us from the sun.

"So," Ann says, like it's a question, "I've been meaning to ask you, do you like Hari now?"

My eyes burst open. "Um, I kind of kissed him last night," I say with the straw still in my mouth.

"What?" Ann spits out her drink and slaps both hands against the picnic table.

"Yeah, I went over there after Birchwood and it just kinda happened. I still can't believe it myself."

Her eyes are bugging out. "And?"

"And, well, it was actually really nice." I feel my whole face redden.

"I can't believe it! But then again, you've liked him for a long time, haven't you . . ."

"I guess so. It's just, I feel happy when I'm around him, and I'm thinking about him when I'm not even around him. It's new territory, you know?"

"Kind of."

"And, what about you?" I gulp my sweet drink.

"Me?"

"Yeah. Do you like Binks? Or someone else? You can tell me. You can tell me anything."

"Well, actually—"

"Yeah?"

"So"—she pauses—"how did you know you liked a *boy*?"

"Well, to be honest, Hari is the first boy I've ever liked, in *that* way."

"But how did you know that you *liked* liked boys, specifically?"

"Oh, right. Okay, well, for me, it really was never a question. That part was always clear." I take another long sip. "But that doesn't mean that's the only answer," I add. "So, I guess that means you don't like Binks, then?"

"No. Definitely not Binks," she answers, giggling.

"Thank goodness, because I definitely would have questioned our friendship on that one."

Ann and I start laughing for an extra-long time. Even the birds fly away from us because we just can't stop laughing.

After we finally calm down I say, "Binks's sister is kinda pretty, though."

"She's *way* cooler than Binks," Ann says.

"Totally."

We cheers our bottles again.

Ann flashes me a huge smile. The biggest smile I've ever seen from her. I smile back with my whole entire heart.

We just have time to finish up our drinks before there's a knock on the window.

"She must be done. Let's get rid of these bottles," I say.

Ann puts them in the red crate by the garbage cans. "Fingers crossed we get something from those photos."

"And toes," I say.

After we finally calm down I say, "Binks's sister is kinda pretty, though."

"Have you cooled off some?" Iris asks.

"Sure did," I say. "Thanks for being so fast."

"You betcha. Now listen, there was a problem with the roll. None of the photos turned out."

"Oh! How so?" Ann reaches over the counter.

"They were pitch-black. It often happens when the film is taken out before the roll is completed. I'll get them to show you what I mean."

She digs them out of the garbage and my heart sinks like a heavy stone. I hold on to the counter to steady myself. She flips through the thin stack of empty darkness. There's nothing to see at all.

"Thanks for trying, Iris," Ann forces out.

"No problemo. They're won't be a charge for these since it's a dud roll."

"Thanks," I reply.

"Enjoy these long summer days. It really is the best time of your life."

I wave the wimpiest goodbye.

"We have absolutely nothing," I say. "Ms. Barry is still indisposed. We have no photos. I have a big fat zero to show my mom. No proof whatsoever. What a waste."

"I'm really sorry, Wolf. I guess it's time I face the music and have that conversation with my parents. I'm gonna head back," she says.

"Okay. Hopefully Brandi and Penny came clean last night. I'm fresh out of ideas."

CHAPTER 41

M om's not home. No car **and no Roger**. Thank
goodness. I unlock the door **and spot a note from**
Mom on the counter:

There's a pizza in the freezer. I won't be home for dinner.
Call Grandma if you need anything. I promise not to
be home late. Mom.

I think about Grandma. I consider calling her, but that, too,
just feels too hard right now. I can't bear to hear the sound of
her tired voice. I don't even bother with the pizza; instead I
climb the stairs to my bedroom.

Everything is different now. Everything is changing. My
grandma, my mom, my friends; nothing is like it used to be.

Why can't it be like before? Saturday mornings with Grandma. Saturday afternoons at Birchwood and sleepovers with my friends. Now, nothing is the same.

I go straight to my closet, like a magnet is pulling me, and I reach up for Poppy's metal lunch box. I rifle through my old journals, birthday cards, special photos and trinkets that I keep tucked away. Like Grandma's photo album, these photos of my family mean so much to me because they bring back so many happy memories from before, when everyone was together, including Poppy. I pinch a photo of Grandma holding a huge pumpkin from her garden. Her cheeks are rosy and her eyes are sparkling. I recall the details from that great harvest party in their backyard with the whole family, celebrating. We were all so happy. I remember how we sang songs by the fire under the moonlight while Grandma played her drum and Poppy played his harmonica. Even Mom got into it and played the spoons with some of the neighbours. We danced until it was long past lights out.

Suddenly, I sit up straight and carefully put everything back inside the lunch box. It was there all along and so downright obvious that I nearly missed it. The pictographs are like these photos, stories from long ago about a family—many families. They tell us so much about how they lived and what they loved and even what they were scared of. In a way, they were the very first photos, and no one has the right to destroy something so special, so extraordinary. It would break my heart if someone took my lunch box filled with memories and destroyed them.

I click the metal box closed and pick up my phone. I dial Ann's number at superhero speed.

"Did you tell them?"

"They're not home."

"Call the girls and meet me at the mountain."

"What are we doing?"

"I know what we have to do, but I can't do it alone. We're saving Birchwood and that mountain, tonight."

I jump on my Supercycle and pedal past the smokestack, spilling its fumes high in the sky, past Kipling Park, past our beloved Birchwood, nestled within the five majestic birch trees. I hide my bike in the bushes and hurry up the gravel road. There are work trucks and lights flashing, several voices booming. I also hear a woman's voice. I realize it's my mom. I'm just about to bust out of my hiding place when the girls arrive behind me.

"Wolf, we're here!"

"Is that your mom, over there with Roger?" Brandi points.

"Yeah. I don't want to talk about her. I'm here to save this mountain."

Penny puts both her hands on both my shoulders. "What do you want us to do?"

"The only way to stop this tonight is to make a human shield. There's no way they'll blast if we're near there. We go and stick our bodies to the mountainside until someone calls for help, and then we show them what we're protecting inside that mountain."

"That sounds extremely risky," Brandi says.

"It is. So I'll understand if you don't want to do it." I look into their eyes. I hold my breath and wait.

"I'm in," Ann says.

"I'm in," Brandi says.

"All in," Penny says. "Let's save these ancient drawings."

"Thank you!" Tears sting my eyes. "On the count of three, we go for it. Okay? Ready?"

I flip one finger, then two, and at three, we rush towards the mountain. My heart soars while I sprint across the gravel. It feels like I'm flying, like my arms are actually wings.

"Hey! There are kids up here!" A man with a hard hat yells out.

"Run!" I scream. "Faster!"

My feet are almost hitting my butt as I race for the mountain. I finally reach the black rock, gripping it with my hands.

"What in the— Wolf!" Roger shouts, approaching us in a reflective vest and large boots. His forehead is furrowed under his hard hat and his eyes are black, shiny nuggets. "Get out of there! Now!" he yells.

"Wolf!" Mom calls. "What are you doing here? You're going to get hurt!"

"I can't believe you're here and you're just letting this happen."

She hurries over and grabs my arms.

"That's not true," she says. "I believe you! That's why I'm here. To talk to Roger."

"You are?"

Her eyes fill with tears. "I came here to see it for myself and I saw them, with my own eyes, and they are absolutely beautiful! You were right, sweetheart."

"You mean you climbed the mountain and you saw the deer and the moose?"

"Yes, and the turtles and thunderbirds. Just like the ones Grandma told me about, so long ago. Irreplaceable painted stories, like the ones our own ancestors painted."

"And Roger?"

"He didn't know. He saw them for the first time tonight, with me."

"But that's not possible. How could he not know?"

"That's what we're trying to find out. But it's dangerous. They were preparing to blast and it's very risky to be here right now. You have to go."

"I can't. I won't. Not until I know this mountain is safe."

"Please," Mom says with fresh tears in her eyes. "Roger called the authorities. He's not blasting the mountain, but the dynamite is still on site."

"He did? He's not? But how could he not know?"

Mom's tears roll down her cheeks. "I don't know, but he wants to protect them too. As soon as he saw them, he shut it down."

I turn to look at Brandi and Penny and Ann, and their faces are just as shocked and confused as mine. Maybe, could it be, that I was wrong about Roger the whole time?

"Please," Mom says, "you all need to step away from the mountain. Dynamite is extremely dangerous. It can combust on its own. You have to listen to me!"

Roger's face is sweaty and his eyes look worried. "Wolf, listen to your mother." He kneels down on one knee and looks me right in the eye. "I promise you that I will personally protect those pictographs. You have my word," he says like he really means it. "I wish you would have told me. But I'm glad we found out before it was too late."

When Roger says that, I get truth bumps, which tells me that he *is* telling me the truth, so I take a slow step forward. The girls follow suit and we hold hands and then we break into a run, away from the mountain. I turn back and watch Roger pointing at his workers and ordering people to move away while he gets the dynamite off the site. I can't believe this is happening. Like everything has been turned inside out.

Roger didn't know. Roger stopped it.

We're rushed to a safer area, away from the zone of impact.

Mom lunges for me. Hugs me. "Everything is going to be okay now."

She kisses my whole face and I can't help but let her. She brings in the girls and we have a huge group hug. We're all so stunned, we haven't been able to say anything yet to each other. We're all wiping our happy tears away when we finally find some words.

"Can you believe this is really over?" Brandi says.

"Understatement of the millennium," Ann says. "We did it."

"We did," I say, letting both happiness and relief wash over me.

Penny leans in. "This is the best day, ever. Am I right?"

"Totally," I say, bursting with bliss.

Out of the corner of my eye, I spot the silhouette of a woman with glasses. "Ms. Barry?" I cry, thankful to finally see her.

"I'm so proud of you girls! Looks like you didn't need me much, after all."

We give her the biggest, happiest hug.

CHAPTER 42

The next day, we give our official statements to the police. And we learn the truth about Roger's head foreman, named Jim, and Detective Belinski, who were working together to keep the pictographs hidden from Roger. I didn't find out all of the details, but it turns out they were in cahoots with one of the developers from Toronto who wanted to keep building in our town. Detective Belinski and the foreman were receiving hush money to keep quiet, so they could keep building.

After leaving the police station, Mom and I go straight to Grandma's. I zip around the backyard and spot her sitting by her garden with a blanket around her, even though it's warm enough to wear shorts.

"It's Cagney & Lacey!" she says. "You two sure know how to get a town talking! Wowsers! Mrs. Mancini filled me in. Her daughter works at the police station, you know."

"It's been quite a couple days," Mom says.

"That's for sure. And where is your Romeo?"

Mom blushes and it actually makes me smile. "He's busy removing his equipment from the work site."

"So does that mean there won't be a new development after all?"

"That's right. There's actually going to be *a lot* of changes around here. We spent the night talking about it."

"Well, I'm excited to hear all about it, Cathy."

"Thanks."

"Wolf, you must be pretty proud of yourself for saving those pictographs."

"I'm glad the truth is out. I just feel bad that I blamed Roger, when he didn't even know about it. And, I'm sorry I waited so long to tell you, Mom." I look down at my feet. "I've been feeling really rotten about it. I also need to apologize to Roger."

Mom reaches over and hugs my shoulder.

"Don't be so hard on yourself," Grandma says. "Even the best investigators get it wrong sometimes. It's good to be remorseful but the important thing is that no one got hurt and that Roger is a good egg after all."

"Yeah," I say.

"Besides, I think you'll have some time to make it up to him, with the upcoming nuptials and all." Grandma winks.

I'm still coming to terms with that, him moving in with us. But for now, it's nice to know that we're all on the same team. Roger did the right thing when he learned about the pictographs. That's a really big deal in my books.

"Well, girls, we have some celebrating to do."

"Mother, you should rest."

"That doesn't mean we can't suck back a couple of colas and have a slice of lemon meringue, does it?"

"I guess not." She reaches over and kisses Grandma's cheek.

I bound up from my lawn chair and sprint to the fridge.

"Put those fancy paper umbrellas in the glasses, they're in the pantry. And use the tray. We're having a party!"

I come back balancing the drinks and the extra-large pieces of pie on the lacquered sunburst tray.

"That's my girl," Grandma shouts from her chair. "So what's the plan, Stan, for the rest of the summer?"

"Well." Mom exhales. "Roger and I have made some big decisions that are going to affect our work schedules." She says it like she can barely hold the words in any longer.

"Spill it," Grandma says, reading my exact thoughts.

"Wolf, it's actually because of you that we've made these changes. We've decided"—she pauses—"we're no longer building and selling new houses." Her eyes grow big and round. She waits for our reaction.

"But what do you mean? What will you do for work?" I ask, completely confused.

"Well, sweetheart, Roger and I are starting a *new* business. We're going to flip old houses together. Fix them up and sell them. He'll do the renovations and I'll do the decorating and selling."

"Well, I'll be!" Grandma smacks her lap. "What a complete turnaround."

"It sure is," Mom says, beaming. "It was actually Roger's idea. He couldn't believe how brave you were about saving those trees and the mountain. He said it woke him up. Like something inside him had been asleep and he had forgotten what really matters. He doesn't want to destroy any more land. He'd rather work on the houses that already exist, and so do I— it woke me up too. We'll make this city beautiful by fixing old houses together."

"Wow, Mom! I can't believe this! It's the best news ever! And it was Roger's idea?"

She wipes her eyes. "It really was."

"Talk about juicy news," Grandma says.

"And . . ." Mom looks like she has something else up her sleeve.

"Do tell." Grandma leans in.

"Besides redecorating Wolf's room." Mom grins the grinniest grin. "I want to make some *other* changes."

Mom drags her chair a little closer to Grandma. She turns so their knees touch. "I've learned some other important things lately." Her voice is a little shaky now and she's looking straight at Grandma. "I'd like to start"—she clears her throat—"start exploring pictographs, especially Algonquin pictographs and other traditions you've wanted to share with me in the past."

"Well, I'll be. This is big-time news, Cathy! I'm as proud as a peacock right now."

"I'm sorry it took me so long to find my way back."

"I knew you would, dear. I really did." Grandma wipes at her tears and reaches for Mom's hand.

They smile twin smiles.

"And, Wolf." She turns to me. "I know how much you've wanted to connect with our culture and I'm sorry for not encouraging that," she says, dabbing her tears. I can tell she wants to say even more but she stops to catch her shaky breath.

I spring to my feet and hug Mom, the kind of hug that says I forgive you and I love you, the super-squishy-squeezy kind. She hugs me back, way longer than three Mississippis.

"We'll make up for all the lost time. I promise," she whispers in my ear.

Once I sit back down, Grandma says, "And, what about you, Wolf?" She scoops up some pie. "What's on your agenda?"

"Well." I exhale. "Besides hanging with you and Mom, I'm just planning on doing regular thirteen-year-old stuff with my friends. You know, looking for UFOs, Bigfoot, the odd sleepover here and there," I answer, trying to keep a straight face.

"That sounds swell. Just swell." Grandma licks her fork.

"No sneaking out, I mean it," Mom says, half serious and half playful. Well, maybe more serious than playful.

"So." Mom lowers her eyes. "What do *you* want to do?" she asks Grandma with a touch of her hand and a sadness in her voice that she can't hide.

Grandma tips her head to the side. "Funny you should ask that. I have some ideas." She winks at me. "Grab me that bag over there, Wolf, the one over by the chaise lounge."

I try to pick it up but it weighs a ton so I decide to drag it over. "Grandma, this is really heavy."

"It better be, it's filled with V.I.B.: Very Important Books that every woman should read. I thought we'd start our very own book club this summer. We can meet every couple of weeks and eat snacks and drink fizzy beverages. We can meet late afternoon or under the stars at night."

"That sounds like fun!"

"Girls only, of course." Her face crinkles with glee. "Are you in, Cathy?"

"Of course I'm in," Mom says, wiping her eyes again.

"Perfecto! I thought we'd start with this beauty." Grandma pulls out *Little Women* by Louisa May Alcott. "Girl power. What do you think?"

"I think it's perfect."

Mom winks at me, and in this very moment, everything *is* perfect.

CHAPTER 43

We're heading to the new park today—the park that was officially supposed to be *Northwood Heights, Subdivision R-6*. The mayor, her councillors and the entire town wanted to help create something beautiful, something meaningful to commemorate the pictographs. They voted unanimously for the city to purchase the land and turn it into a special park where visitors can come and see the pictographs.

This time next year, the park will be ready for the public, but today they are doing a special commemoration with the Anishinaabe elders who have been asked to bless the land through a traditional smudging ceremony. Grandma and Mom are here, and the pack. We've been invited as special guests.

Roger is here as well. He arrived separately because he went to cut Grandma's lawn and work her garden for her. It's still a little weird sometimes, having him around all the time, and even weirder that in less than three months, he's going to be my stepfather. But I can tell he wants us to be a family. He loves buying things in packs of threes, which are hard to find because most things come in packs of four. It's become something we like to do together, like a treasure hunt. We've also been creating our own traditions with Roger, like Tuesday taco nights and Friday movie nights at the drive-in. Another thing we do together is rummage through antique shops on Sunday mornings. We always leave bright and early, and it's never hard to get up on those days.

It's actually been okay, maybe even more than okay. Roger's not living with us yet, but he started moving some of his things into the basement. It's not as bad as I thought it would be. It's kind of great, because Mom is really happy.

He's walking towards me right now, waving me down. I meet him halfway. "So," he says, "it's a big day today." His feet shift under him. He's still a little shy around me sometimes, especially when Mom isn't with us.

"It is. Really big. I still can't believe how much has happened this summer," I say.

"You and me both." He wipes his brow.

"Um, I'm still really sorry, for how all that went down."

"You already apologized, several times now. And I already forgave you, remember?"

"I know, but I want to make sure you know how much I mean it."

"All right. Message received. Let's just say, we *all* learned some important lessons this summer, okay?"

"Okay."

"Good. That's really good." He nods his head up and down. "Hey, you're wearing the necklace." He points to the pendant around my neck.

"Yeah, I thought it was the perfect day to wear it." I smile and pinch it between my fingers.

He smiles back and his eyes get a little shimmery. "Okay then," he says, "go on now and find your friends, and Wolf—"

"Yeah?"

"I'm real proud of you and I feel lucky that I'm going to be your stepdad."

My face lights up like a Christmas tree.

Supposedly, the mayor found out about our nature research through Ann's mom. They've since created a resource binder with all of the information we collected. You can now read *The Birchwood Records* in the reference-only section at the library. Ms. Barry helped us organize it. It's on the Must-Read Summer List. She says it's brought in many new curious readers of all ages. The library hasn't been so quiet since all of the news broke out. Nothing is the same around here, and I guess that's a good thing.

After the very special smudging ceremony, we planted a new tree. A yellow birch. The council asked us what kind of tree we wanted to plant and I knew without a single doubt that it had to be this one. I'm still not a tree talker like my great-granddaddy, at least not yet. I can't hear what they say but I believe they can hear me. I hope they know how much they mean to me and how I'll always protect them. I want everyone to have a chance to see this tree grow big and tall, like the ones my great-granddaddy protected so long ago.

"Wolf!" Ann yells from one of the benches. Penny's waving me over too. Did you see this?"

"See what?"

"The bench? Our names are on it, engraved on the plaque. See?"

"Wow! That's so cool!" I touch it and read the words:

Wolf, Ann, Brandi, Penny: In honour of their courage.

Ann points to the next line: *Forever Birchwood.*

"I told my mom to add that part," Ann says. "It's amazing how you get your way when your parents tell you they're separating."

"I'm sorry, Ann," Penny says.

"Yeah, me too. I wish you weren't moving," I tell her.

"I know. But Mom says I'll really like Ottawa. There are a ton of museums there and I especially want to see the Museum of Civilization."

"It does sound perfect for you," I say.

"Hey, guys!" Brandi waves.

I call her over. "So, Timmins, right? I'm still in denial that you're leaving."

"I know. Me too. Dad says he's trading in nickel for gold. My grandparents still live up there, so I'm looking forward to spending time with them again. I'm going to miss you guys, though. Horribly."

"I'm really going to miss you too," Penny says.

Brandi leans her head on Penny's shoulder.

"I guess Esmeralda was right," I say. "Everything *is* different now." I try not to let my voice shake.

"That night feels like another lifetime ago," Brandi answers.

"Yup," Ann says. "We're all going our own separate ways."

"But aren't you and Penny going to the same school?" Brandi turns towards me.

"No, actually," Penny replies. "I've decided to go to Marymount. It's all girls, and I want to steer clear of boys for now and concentrate on getting good grades. I have my sights on university biology," she says. "I learned a lot about myself this summer and it turns out I love science. Especially plants." She smirks.

"Super plan," I tell her.

"And you, Wolf? What are your plans?" Penny asks.

I shrug. "Honestly, I don't even want to think about high school right now. With Grandma Houle being sick and all, sometimes I feel like I just want time to stop."

"You're going to Ridgewood High, though, right? Just like Hari?" Brandi asks. Her face glows like a firefly.

"Yeah, I'm pretty sure." I feel my cheeks warm and then my eye catches a sparkle in the distance. The newly planted yellow birch shimmers in the bright afternoon sun and my heart sings.

"So, should we meet one last time at Birchwood tonight?" I ask.

"All in," they say.

ACKNOWLEDGEMENTS

Middle grade is my absolute happy place.

This novel has been the most fun I've ever had writing, but it still wasn't easy. I'm grateful to so many people and so many bright hearts, and I'm delighted to finally have the opportunity to thank them here, because without them, this book would not exist.

Big thanks to my Children's Literature MFA classmates at the University of British Columbia, who supported this story when I first began. Your feedback encouraged me to keep going. Special thanks to Cara Violini and Jill MacKenzie for reading early drafts of this novel, and to Claire Arnett for her heartfelt encouragement long after class ended. Thank you to Alison Acheson and Maggie de Vries for making me believe it was possible and for not trying to convince me to set it in present time.

Warm thanks to the many kind writers at the Firefly Creative Writing retreat, where I wrote the first twenty-five pages inside a cozy cottage on the shores of Georgian Bay. Wolf and Grandma Houle were born in your safe haven. (Oh, those delicious meals!) Your enthusiasm and support gave me wings.

Very special thanks to Kelly Sonnack, my agent extraordinaire, who believed in me and this story long before it was ready to submit. Thank you for pushing me and for championing my book the way you did. I'm so glad we found each other.

A big thank-you to my editor, Suzanne Sutherland, for the way you embraced this novel with so much heart and care. I knew without a doubt this story belonged in your hands. I'm ever grateful for your kind support. To Iris Tupholme, Noelle Zitzer and the entire team at HarperCollins Canada, who so enthusiastically welcomed me into their publishing family, thank you for choosing this novel, and to Catherine Dorton, for her thoughtful copy edits. I'm incredibly grateful to each and every one of you for helping me put this book into the world!

Thank you to Liisa Kovala for our monthly coffee meet-ups, walks in the woods and many weekends writing on Manitoulin Island, and for incessantly talking about writing with me.

To Melanie Hunt, a million thank-yous for being there for all the good times and all the hard times, and for letting me talk your ear off as I tried to fix plot issues for the umpteenth time. I would be lost without you.

ACKNOWLEDGEMENTS

Loving thanks to my dear mom, for always believing in me and cheering me on through every storm, and for telling me I was a writer long before it was true.

To Steve and Owen, my Loves, my everything, thank you for sharing every loss and every win. Thank you for supporting this writing thing.

To my dear readers, thank you for embracing my stories, for holding them so carefully and sharing them with your friends and loved ones over the years. Truly and sincerely.

To the land in which I was born and raised—to the trees, the mountains, the lakes and every living creature—I give loving thanks. I am who I am because of the medicine and shelter you have provided me. I promise to keep showing up and keep listening.

Danielle XO